The Weighing of the Heart

Paul Tudor Owen

The Weighing of the Heart
Copyright © 2019 Paul Tudor Owen

Published by Obliterati Press 2019

www.obliteratipress.com

ISBN: 978-1-9997528-4-2

The Weighing of
the Heart

Chapter 1

Sooner or later, everybody comes to New York, and I was no exception. For me, it was art school that brought me over, and I left behind the brash primary colours of late-90s London gladly and without remorse. Here I could reinvent myself, as others had before me, among the shining slabs of a city that seemed to have scale where others only had size, where history was measured in the minutes rather than the centuries, and where each of its ten million inhabitants began their lives anew each morning when they awoke and pulled up the blinds. After college I did everything I could to remain, winning a job and the work permit that came with it at the Bougainville Gallery in Chelsea, and spending the next few years living in a tiny apartment in Greenpoint with my girlfriend Hannah, working together at the gallery each day and growing gradually further and further apart.

In early spring in 2011, things finally came to a

head, and I moved out, for reasons I don't really want to go into here. I left, and went to stay on the couch of a former colleague in whom I'd increasingly been confiding. His name was not Jeff, but I have to give him a name and Jeff will do as well as any other. Hannah's name wasn't really Hannah either.

Jeff had two aunts who lived uptown in one of those huge late-nineteenth-century apartment blocks where wealthy families often take up a whole floor. Their apartment was enormous, sprawling, Jeff said, with an elegant roof garden looking out in a wide panorama over Central Park. But it was also ragged and unloved, and slowly rotting away; his aunts only lived there two days a week, spending the rest of their time at their other home on Long Island. To make sure the place didn't collapse completely they usually took in a lodger, and as luck would have it, Jeff told me, they needed one right now. Since I was desperate to find somewhere to live, he would take me round to meet them and we could see whether we hit it off.

Far from being desperate to find somewhere to live, I was in fact quite enjoying my evenings in his apartment in Clinton Hill watching reality TV with his witty and outspoken girlfriend Severin, whose parents had named her after the character in the Velvet Underground song 'Venus in Furs'. But I am a very suggestible person, and I must admit that as Jeff and I talked about it more, I found myself drifting off into an agreeable fantasy about life in that cavernous apartment a stone's throw from Central Park – the white whorl of the Guggenheim visible from the living room window, MoMA, the Met – and I began to feel really quite excited about the whole idea. For the five days each week when the Peacock sisters would be away I would have the whole palatial penthouse to myself, and it was pleasant to feel even in a vague and materialistic sense that I would be making some progress in my life after my break-up with Hannah, which I felt had set me back a step as the rest of my friends busied themselves getting married, getting pregnant, getting comfortably settled in for the next stage of life.

So I went up there with Jeff and Severin after work the next Wednesday, Severin boasting during the subway ride that the sisters viewed her as 'the daughter they never had', and they introduced me to Marie and Rose Peacock. We all had a glass of California red, and Marie and Rose took me on a quick whirl around the apartment – including the small bedroom beside the roof garden that would be mine. Then it was time for the Peacocks to leave for the theatre and we all took the lift down to the street. As Jeff flagged them down a cab, Marie Peacock asked me a few questions about my job, tugged thoughtfully at her coat cuffs, peered into my eyes, and abruptly proposed rent of a hundred dollars a week, a sum so minuscule for the Upper East Side she might as well have made it one peppercorn. I couldn't shake her hand fast enough.

"We've been looking for a lodger for a while now," she told me, as we sheltered from the spring breeze under the building's awning.

"A year or two, off and on, since the last one," put in Rose.

"We like to have someone we know..." continued Marie.

"Someone we know, or a friend of a friend..."

"Or a friend of a nephew!" said Marie, waving a gloved hand in Jeff's direction. "So it often takes us a while to find the right person."

"The last young man painted the bedroom walls green," Rose recalled mournfully.

"I think we'll say no painting the walls this time," decided Marie. "Is that all right, young man?"

"Of course," I said.

"You can move in tomorrow if you like," added Rose, as Jeff held open the cab door.

So I did.

*

They gave me a more detailed tour when I brought round my belongings the next evening. The building had been constructed in 1878, they told me. Marty Gamble lived next door, if I was interested in comedy, and somebody who once ran for president for the Constitution Party was on the ground floor. The apartment had been in the family for generations. Marie Peacock, the younger aunt, had never lived anywhere else, having taken over the running of the place aged just twenty-five after her parents had died. Rose, her elder sister, had moved back in following her divorce twenty years ago. That small refrigerator in the corner of the kitchen was mine, they said, and I shouldn't use theirs; the same went for the telephone.

"If it rings, don't answer it," Marie said. "The voicemail will pick it up. And please don't let anyone in unless you are expecting someone. If somebody is downstairs and you don't know who they are, do not under any circumstances buzz them up. We own a number of properties around the city, young Nicholas, and there have been some... difficult incidents over the years, as I'm sure you can imagine. So don't give anyone your name. And certainly don't give them our names. As I always tell my nephew: the only people you are legally obliged to let into your home are uniformed police."

It was clear from the off that the sisters were a slightly eccentric pair, but I was more than willing to take the rough with the smooth – for example, the phenomenally low rent.

My room was on the lower of the Peacocks' one-and-a-half floors; upstairs were the sisters' bedrooms, and Rose's library – she was a retired university professor who had specialised, she told me, in cultural representations of sex. Between their bedrooms, steps led up to a tiny attic crawlspace full of old paintings, papers and bedding which Marie jokingly (I think) referred to as 'the butler's room'. Their cat, Francine, who accompanied them to and from Water Mill, NY, each week, looked up lazily from a stained mattress as we opened the door, and Rose indulgently scrabbled at the back of its neck. "Hello, Frannie!"

Through the kitchen at the back of the apartment was a laundry room that opened out down a few iron steps on to the roof garden, and across the garden at the far side was a bare-looking door.

"Now," said Marie. "I hope Rose has mentioned young Lydia?" She had not. Marie pointed across the roof garden. "Young Lydia is our other tenant; she lives in the apartment across the roof there. Husband used to live there too, but they went their separate ways some months ago, I'm sorry to say. Very sad; lovely young man. Her apartment is totally self-contained, but we do give her a key to this utility room here so she can do her laundry."

"No sense her throwing her paycheck away down at the laundromat, poor thing," put in Rose.

"So if you come in here and find a beautiful girl washing her underwear – don't panic!" Marie concluded with a hearty laugh. I laughed too. The more I learned about this strange set-up the more enthusiastic I felt.

And then they left for Long Island, and it was a spooky old place without them. Jeff had joked that my role would lie somewhere between tenant and night watchman, and indeed that night as I struggled to get to sleep, feeling as tiny and insignificant as a speck of dust drifting across this vast expanse, I heard a rattling at the back door, and jumped out of bed, shaken, silently opened my blinds a crack, and looked out across the roof garden through the darkness.

It was Lydia, letting herself in to the Peacocks' apartment with a basket of laundry propped at her hip. I watched her open the laundry room door and disappear inside, invisible at my darkened window, and then watched again as she came out a few minutes later, ducking slightly under the light spring rain. She was very pretty, her long, wavy brown hair gathered in a flattering fashion at the nape of her neck, her eyes gleaming in the reflected light from the laundry room like a cat's. She was wearing shorts and Converse trainers and a diaphanous red tank-top, and I watched her as she disappeared back into her apartment, and I went back to bed wondering about the next time she would sneak quietly across the roof, thinking about Marie Peacock's words: "If you come in here and find a beautiful girl in her underwear doing her laundry – don't panic!"

And so life settled into a rhythm, as lives quickly do. On Wednesdays, the Peacock sisters would arrive from Long Island, often with friends, former colleagues, or relatives in tow, and that night and the next I would spend my evenings out seeing friends, or stay late working on my paintings at a studio space I shared with some other artists in Bushwick. When the Peacock sisters were home they were everywhere; I could be opening a parcel in the hallway, believing myself completely alone, when Rose would noiselessly appear, murmur "Exotic..." in a wondering tone as she surveyed my delivery and then melt away mysteriously into the living room, the rustle of her elegant evening dress disappearing after her. In the kitchen, Marie would be sitting at the table with a cup of coffee, her hennaed hair glowing in the pale evening sun, and would put down her glasses and her Wall Street Journal to ask me detailed questions about my life so far: where I grew up, what my school was like, my jobs, my ambitions, and compare them to her own, to her brother's, to her nephew's, to those of the Peacock family's distant and hazily-imagined Dutch ancestors – sometimes favourably, sometimes unfavourably. The two of them thought of me, it emerged, as someone who had 'made his way up out of the gutter', by which I think they probably meant anywhere south of 59th Street and north of 88th rather than England in particular. I think they rather liked me because of it.

I avoid reminiscing, as a rule, but the Peacock sisters did manage to get a few recollections out of me during those early conversations: details about my uninspiring comprehensive school, my drab group of childhood friends, my parents – who had always admired my artwork and encouraged me to pursue the subject, but had received a bit of a shock when they discovered that I had scorned the Slade, the RCA, Goldsmiths and the rest and had applied instead to the New York Academy of Art, calculating that the inheritance my grandfather had left me would just about cover the fees. We argued back and forth – they had assumed I would put the money towards a flat – but in the end what could they do? I was eighteen and it was my money.

What appealed to me about New York was what appealed to me about art itself – it was a place where I could pretend that the gloomy half-light of my hometown, the exhausted indistinguishable streets stretching out endlessly into the void, had quite simply never existed; where I could decide who I was and who I wanted to be and nobody would ever be able to challenge it. It was the place of Rothko and Rockwell and Hopper and Pollock and Warhol, the names that I hoped to join and perhaps one day surpass – although obviously I didn't tell the Peacocks that.

So the sisters got to know a little about me, and I a little about them: Rose, the older sister, was quieter, more thoughtful; Marie had a better sense of humour. Rose got up early and Marie went to bed late. Marie handled the family finances; Rose was in charge of their extensive and varied social life. A year or two had passed since they had last had a lodger, and they were well used to their own company. Once, early on, I was sitting reading by the window in the living room when I became aware that Marie had materialised beside me.

"I don't have many rules, young man..." she began untruthfully.

"But this is your chair?" I guessed.

"But that is my chair," she said.

I stood up reluctantly and crossed to the sofa.

*

And on Fridays, when I arrived home from work, the sisters would be gone, and the place would be mine for the rest of the week. I bounced around the enormous rooms like a pinball.

I cooked basic meals in the kitchen, on one occasion slicing open a red pepper to see a small, colourless moth fly out, whirl woozily in the air and then collapse on the floorboards, spent. I tried not to think of it as a metaphor.

I drew at my desk, amassing stacks of pencil sketches that I filed carefully in plastic binders on the shelf above my wardrobe. The walls were thin, and I could sometimes hear Lydia in her apartment next door, doing whatever, taking a shower.

Crammed into one small bedroom, I resigned myself to gradually having to transport around a third of my possessions to downtown thrift stores, where hipsters could loot them to their hearts' content: clothes, CDs, records, books. I gave away a glass chessboard my father had presented me with on the day of my GCSE results, and even briefly considered throwing out an even more prized possession, my grandmother's ancient wooden Scrabble set, before deciding that that was where I would draw the line.

I got to meet Marty Gamble after a fashion when a parcel of his was wrongly delivered to my mailbox, and he turned out to be as unsmiling in his way as the 'tears of a clown' comedian of popular myth, opening the door just a crack with a cellphone clamped to his ear, a wire-haired dachshund tangling itself up at his ankles, a sullen scowl disfiguring his face.

"Yeah?" he asked me rudely, only breaking off from his telephone conversation to yell "Down, Bruiser!" at the dog as it lunged aggressively towards me.

"I live next door," I said. "This package came for you."

"Thanks," he said, grabbing it. "Yeah, just some guy with the mail," he told the phone as he closed the door.

Jeff and Severin came by and showed me the pencil marks on the kitchen door where Jeff and his sisters had measured their heights as children, the storage unit where his aunts kept their air rifle, and the pellet holes that Jeff had made in the hallway walls with it as a teenager. I spent a satisfying evening fixing the broken doors of the cupboards the

Peacock sisters had allocated to me, and went to bed with superglue on my fingers, unable to feel the pages of the book I was reading. One morning soon after moving in I came wandering into the kitchen to find a small Korean woman in her mid-forties washing the dishes.

"Hyo-Sonn – cleaner," she said, pointing to herself, and I was so disorientated I could only reply, "Nick Braeburn – lodger."

In the evenings, voicemail messages would beep to themselves in the living room in a lonely fashion, waiting for the Peacocks to come home and pick them up, making the room essentially uninhabitable unless the TV or the radio was turned up loud enough to drown them out.

I had never lived in a place that made so many 'house sounds' before: unsettling creaks and rumbles, rattles, clicks and sighs, the walls and doorframes expanding and contracting like bellows. I often had violent dreams, woke up fighting childhood bullies or burglars; I'm sure there was a connection. When I was a child, our house was broken into a number of times, which was not unusual for our part of south-east London but which nonetheless left a strong impression on me, and that helpless feeling of knowing somebody had invaded the space that belonged to us, the space

17

where we ought to have felt ourselves completely safe, returned to me often during the lonely nights of those first few weeks at the Peacocks'. One evening when the sisters were away I was close to falling asleep when I heard a huge crash coming from somewhere on my floor or the one above, as if a stack of videotapes had fallen over or somebody had slammed a cupboard door. I rushed out of my room in my boxer shorts yelling, "Hello? Hello?" and stood there in the hallway, a cold breeze lapping unaccountably at my ankles, moths and motes of dust rising in the air around me, and then I nervously and systematically searched every corner of every room, except for their study, which they always kept locked when they were away. But nothing, and I went back to bed feeling a bit defenceless, leaving a lamp on in an embarrassingly effective gesture of childlike reassurance.

That was the first time I had had a proper look at the Peacocks' bedrooms, which lay peacefully in benign disarray, like a sleeping sidewalk hobo. Stray pillows were strewn across the floor, quarter-drunk cups of coffee sat on the nightstands. Hyo-Sonn was obviously the type of cleaner who had a strict 'no tidying' rule. Blinds were pulled down and drawers left open, and a pair of hair straighteners had been left plugged in and were branding their silhouette into Rose's floorboards (I pulled out the plug).

But I had been surprised when I got up there to find that the sisters seemed to have a keen interest in contemporary art: a Fernando Botero print hung beside Marie's mirror, and above her chest of drawers was one of Sarah Morris's origami beetles. In Rose's room, one of John Squire's Alhambra-style patterns, meant to represent the personalities of celebrities and murderers, hung by the wardrobe and by the window was a vertiginous squiggle by Martin Samarkos, with whom I went to art school and whose personality, believe me, is almost as astonishingly dull as his art. I was just about to take a closer look when my eye fell on a hand-painted birthday card in a frame beside Rose's bed: a small papyrus-style painting of the Barque of Ra, the boat in which the Ancient Egyptian sun-god travelled through the sky by day and through the Netherworld by night.

I stopped, surprised. My own artwork was all about Ancient Egypt, and I had painted a very similar scene myself a couple of years earlier. But I had to admit it: this was a really impressive attempt. The curve of the barque had been established confidently with little more than two or three lines. The Field of Reeds, the afterlife in the east towards which the boat was heading, seemed lush, verdant, a place so warm, welcoming and alive it was hard to credit that it had anything to do with death. Ra was depicted twice, once in his falcon-headed form as Ra-Horakhty and once with the head of a scarab as Khepri, and above him the artist had worked the sun in thick, wet strokes that glimmered and glittered so brightly I was almost afraid to look at it, as if it would burn my eyes out if I stared too long. I felt quite jealous, and I thought about the little painting often in my studio in the days that followed.

An Englishman in New York is not an exotic thing, but on the Upper East Side my countrymen seemed more common than ever. I encountered them in coffee shops and offices, on magazine covers and billboards, behind the bar in swanky restaurants or in front of the bar in 'Irish' 'pubs'. On one occasion in a shoe shop, it gradually dawned on me that not only were all the customers English, all the staff were too. I took off the shoe I had been trying on and left as soon as it was polite to do so.

I bought expensive groceries at D'Agostino's, eavesdropping on the bickering staff and waiting in the queue on one occasion behind Marty Gamble, who looked haggard and harassed and cut out of line at the last minute to pick up twelve bottles of a lethal-looking energy drink.

I signed up with a local squash club, but rather

ruined things on my first day when I arrived early and, to kill time, headed up to the balcony to watch one of the other matches; I must have drifted off somewhat, because after a short while I realised the game had stopped and I was simply staring at two exhausted guys leaning against a wall gulping down bottled water. One of them glanced up at me uncomfortably and I made a swift exit.

I saw Lydia out on the roof garden sometimes, talking on her cellphone in an unfamiliar language, or braving the cold to sit in a garden chair in a thick winter coat reading and smoking, a cup of coffee resting beside her on the short wall at the edge of the roof. I watched her from my room as I pretended to use my laptop. Once she looked up, saw me and gave me a wave, and I waved awkwardly back and quickly retreated further inside. Once she was out there with a tall, Hispanic-looking guy, leaning against the wall of her apartment and smoking. Their faces inclined together as they chatted, relaxed in one another's company, and I thought it was probably her boyfriend, or at the very least she was sleeping with him. She shielded her eyes from the spring sunlight as she spoke, and I could see that Marie Peacock hadn't been joking: she really was very beautiful.

Behind her stretched the park and the monoliths of Midtown like packs of cards set on end, and far in the distance the tip of the construction crane at the top of the new World Trade Center glinted like a diamond. And not for the first time I wondered whether being here in this city on the day the predecessors of that half-built building were destroyed had marked the point when I had begun to stop being English and had started the gradual process of becoming an American.

Some nights rain rattled against the windows like someone was throwing pebbles, and the water in the bathroom gurgled softly like somebody singing. Some nights I leaned out over the edge of the flat roof and watched phones hover like fireflies in the streets below, and car headlamps glitter on the Queensboro Bridge. Some nights neon swam and shimmered in the puddles on the pavement – a simple effect, common the world over, that now whenever I think of it instantly evokes New York. Some nights I went out on my own to eat after work, and watched other men eating alone too, facing no one across a table for two, the waitress tactfully whisking away the cutlery and glass and napkin of their non-existent companions.

I worked constantly and late. I finished paintings and photographed them and adjusted the colour balance on Photoshop and wrote descriptions of my work and artistic philosophy and sent emails to galleries and studios and magazines. I suppose I thought that if I carried on reaching out to this city, if I carried on giving so much, eventually it would give something back. But it never did.

I went to my old apartment to get the last of my things. Hannah had moved out two weeks earlier, our lease was up at the end of the month, and there were cobwebs in the corners of the hallway when I opened the door. Looking through the cupboards one last time, I saw that she'd left behind a hand-painted plate I'd bought her during a trip we'd once taken to Boston, and that had some level of emotional effect on me.

Unfortunately, I had lost my job soon after we had broken up, the gallery owner taking Hannah's side about the whole thing and consequently making things rather difficult for me. The result was that a number of doors that had once seemed open to me in my career were now shut, but I had at least managed to find a new position more or less straight away, at the Latza Art Space around the corner from one of the big Manhattan courthouses between Chinatown and Tribeca. It wasn't as prestigious as the Bougainville, but then again, what is? And although I don't believe in fate or any of that nonsense, there followed a happy coincidence when soon after moving in to the Peacocks' I was in the lobby of the building waiting for the elevator when who should struggle in off the rainy sidewalk but Samuel Latza, my new boss, followed by two wheezing porters carrying five or six suitcases. He had only been into the gallery two or three times since I'd started working there, but evidently he at least dimly recognised me because when I said hello he stopped walking and somehow managed to conjure up my name. I gestured to his bags and his entourage and asked if he was moving into the building.

"Yes," he murmured. "Place on the fifth floor... Lovely part of town... Kids to the park..."

"Yes," I said. "I love being so close to the park myself. I live up on the top floor."

He looked blank, then astonished, and it was clear he was mentally composing a furious email to his general manager to ask him what the hell he was paying gallery assistants these days that they could afford to live on the top floor of mansion blocks on the Upper East Side, and I was just about to put him out of his misery and explain my peculiar living arrangements when the bell rang and the elevator stopped at his floor.

*

One Wednesday night, no one could sleep. I could hear one of the Peacocks creeping about upstairs, floorboards creaking, and as I lay with my ear pressed to the pillow, the pipes seemed to hiss like police sirens. I got up to get a drink from the kitchen and, glancing out the window towards the buildings on the other side of 77th Street before I put the light on, saw two squares of light reflected in the plate-glass windows opposite. I tried to orient myself. The kitchen faced the same way as Lydia's apartment, so the squares were probably her living room and bedroom windows, and just as I had worked that out, I saw the reflection of a female figure glide into view: it was Lydia, wearing only a towel. As I watched she took the towel off, put it carefully on the back of a chair, walked naked to her wardrobe to get her nightdress, and drew the blinds. I stood there watching the blank panel of light for a long time hoping somehow that she'd come back into view.

Chapter 2

In an attempt to get myself socialising again I went out to a nightclub in Bed-Stuy with two friends, Caitlin and Marissa, hoping I wouldn't run into Hannah, who I had heard on the grapevine had moved into a room above a shoe shop on Franklin Avenue. I felt old at the club; Caitlin wanted me to try a new drug I'd never heard of, 'BZP', and somehow it depressed me that it had such a business-like name and that kids nowadays evidently no longer felt the need to come up with evocative, ambrosial nicknames like 'ecstasy', 'hash' or 'speed' for their narcotics. Even ecstasy, it emerged, had now devolved into the more prosaic-sounding MDMA, although Caitlin told me that some people called mephedrone 'bath salts', and I was pleased to hear that, although embarrassingly I had never heard of mephedrone either.

The BZP got us dancing and kept us awake, which is about the minimum you can ask of any drug, and when we got bored with the club I invited the girls back to the Peacocks', where the pills seemed to morph into a sort of truth serum and we spent the next three hours fervidly recounting traumatic memories from our youth and crying on each other's shoulders. At about 5 a.m., after I had finished a long story about a burglar, we all crashed out, Caitlin and I on the two sofas in the lounge and Marissa in my room.

I was just saying goodbye to Caitlin at the front door in the morning when I heard a noise from the laundry room; I peered down the hallway and Lydia emerged from the gloom, a middle-aged man in a workman's cap and blue short-sleeved shirt behind her.

"Nick? Are you in? Oh! I'm sorry," she said abruptly, coming to an awkward halt when she saw Caitlin. "I'm sorry, Nick, it's – The repairman wanted to – I'll come back..."

She had a heavy accent but I couldn't quite place it. "No, no, don't worry," I said weakly. "Come in..."

Caitlin gave me a sleepy goodbye kiss on the cheek and stumbled away towards the elevator, and I closed the door behind her and turned back to Lydia.

"The repairman just wanted to take a look at the heat pipes up here," she was saying, heading towards the kitchen and avoiding my eyes. "They're connected to mine somehow..."

I tried to reply to her, but my mind was as cold and shiny as an empty bathtub from the drug and attendant lack of sleep, and all I could manage was a croaked-out: "Okay..."

"Sorry to interrupt you," Lydia continued. "I should have called before I came over."

At that point, a girl's voice floated forlornly out of my room at the end of the hallway and cut her short.

"Nick..." it moaned.

Lydia stopped talking and looked at me directly for the first time, her eyebrows raised in surprise. She glanced towards my bedroom, then towards the front door, through which Caitlin had disappeared only moments before, and I could see she was now trying hard not to grin.

"I can see we've come at the wrong time," Lydia said, smiling openly now as Marissa materialised in my doorway, make-up smeared, hair recalcitrant and wild, my robe wrapped imperfectly around her body. There was a moment of silence.

"May I have a glass of water?" Marissa asked everyone.

"I think I'd better leave you to it," Lydia said to me, retreating back into the laundry room with the repairman in tow, her eyes glittering with amusement. The door slammed behind them, and I could hear her peppering him with heating-related questions as they made their way back across the roof and I poured Marissa a drink.

*

One of Jeff's sisters, introduced to me as 'young Annabel', had come to stay for a fortnight from Indonesia, where she lived with her husband and their three small children. I was unwell when she arrived, and it turned out to be a very bad week to stay home sick: millions of Peacocks of all ages roamed the apartment: children, babies, parents, cousins, grandchildren, grandchildren's friends. I escaped them, braved the elements and went across to Greenpoint to see my doctor. He told me he could prescribe something for me, but it wouldn't work with my regular medication so I would need to switch to something else instead of that for right now. He asked me if I had ever taken 'neurpraxin'; I didn't think I had.

"Well," he said, "come back to me if it causes any drowsiness or headaches."

He was always ridiculously cautious, which in some ways I quite liked, but, really, there had been no problems like that for a very long time.

When I got back home, laughter and ragtime

music were coming from the open study door, and one of the Peacock sisters shouted down the hallway that I should come in and join them all for some champagne to celebrate young Annabel's temporary return to the United States. I walked in to find the whole family there, including Jeff, Severin, and Jeff's parents, knocking back drinks and discussing in great detail the problems of south-east Asia, about which, it transpired, many of the Peacocks had some decidedly un-PC views.

I hadn't been in the study before; it was always locked when the sisters went away. Like their bedrooms, it had a rumpled, untamed appearance, books crammed into shelves upside down or on end, African statuettes, Native American trinkets, and an open, road-trip-size bottle of mineral water below the gilt-edged mirror on the fireplace. Standard lamps, record players and yellowing birthday cards rounded out the scene, and between the two large windows facing Central Park were two ornate Americana-style banjos. While their bedrooms were devoted to contemporary art, the study walls were a love letter to the twentieth century, with prints by giants such as Roy Lichtenstein, Alex Katz and Marie Laurencin – and to my surprise, another Egyptian link, 'The Weighing of the Heart' by Edward Hazlemere. Before I could take a proper look at it, someone handed me a champagne flute and Marie proposed a toast to young Annabel and the three kids. Finding myself sitting next to Severin I mischievously asked her if she was planning to become Severin Peacock one day. She put her hand on her heart and replied mock-dreamily, "Oh, I hope so..."

"Well, here's to that too!" Marie broke in with un-ironic and infectious enthusiasm, and so we all drank to that too.

"Do you play the banjo?" I asked Marie.

"Play the what now?" she said.

"Those 'duelling banjos'..." I said, gesturing to the wall.

"Oh!" she replied, instantly mellowing.

"You always were soft-hearted, Marie," Rose put in fondly, anticipating her sister's coming remarks.

"Well, *there's* a story," Marie said. "Young Nicholas, as you know we let out a number of properties around the city, and we rented one little studio apartment down on the Lower East Side to a young musician, and, being not the world's most successful musician, he couldn't always make the rent, poor thing."

"So Marie would let him give payment in kind," said Rose.

"He'd give us all sorts of things," Marie said,

chuckling. "Once he gave us a stack of Diana Ross CDs *this* high. And once he gave us a banjo." She corrected herself, looking at the wall: "Twice he gave us a banjo."

"Now, Marie, don't you go giving young Nicholas any ideas," Rose said, and everybody laughed.

Poor thing indeed, I thought; he was never going to make the rent if the Peacocks kept taking possession of all his musical instruments. And they must have known that... but then the banjos did look very impressive up there on their study walls.

They lapsed into planning that year's family Christmas, with much speculation on whether young Vivian, Jeff's eldest sister, absent tonight, would be successfully prevailed upon to make the trip up to Water Mill this year, and I took the opportunity to get a closer look at the Hazlemere print above the Peacocks' desk.

'The Weighing of the Heart' was one of Hazlemere's earliest works, from the late 1950s, if I remembered rightly, when he was still using his signature combination of photography, painting and screenprint. The picture showed an image I knew well: the Day of Judgment for a dead Egyptian, the moment when his guilt or innocence was weighed up and it was decided whether or not he would be allowed to enter the afterlife. A small baboon sat on top of a pair of black scales with which Anubis, the god of embalming with the inky head of a jackal, was measuring the dead man's heart against the weight of an ostrich feather. To their right, Thoth, the god of knowledge and writing, stood ready to record the verdict, the curved beak of his ibis head almost touching the brush with which he would write out the judgment. And waiting hungrily in the background was the Devourer – that appalling, nightmarish beast that was part-lioness, part-crocodile, and part-hippopotamus. If the heart was heavier than the feather, the Devourer would be allowed to eat it, and its bulging pupils seemed to push down the heart's side of the scales with monstrous desire.

It was a fabulous print, reconfirming in my mind the brilliance of Hazlemere, whose work I'd studied at university, but which I had not thought about for some time. The heart had been tinted silver, in an intriguing expressionist touch, while the Devourer's body was carefully sculpted so that the transition from hippopotamus's legs to lion's body to crocodile's head looked not ridiculous but chilling, terrifying even, its eyes baleful and glistening; no mercy there. It loomed over the room like a warning.

*

The weather was starting to turn sunny, and I waited out most of young Annabel's visit on the roof garden, reading and convalescing. One afternoon when I was out there, Lydia's door swung open and she poked her head around it and hissed across to me in a stage whisper, "What's going on over there, Nick? Have Annabel and the kids moved in for good?"

I put down my book. "They're here till next Wednesday," I said.

"How are you coping?" she asked, with a likeable combination of mock and real sympathy, making her way out to sit down on the garden chair next to mine. She was wearing a turquoise skirt and a man's loose white shirt. "I can hear them day and night," she said. "Marie and Rose seem to be there 24/7 at the moment, too."

"Yes," I said. "I've been spending a lot of time out here on the roof."

"Oh dear..." she said, crossing her legs. At that point, one of Annabel's kids came running out of the laundry room, chased by another one, and they circled round Lydia's chair for a moment before rushing back inside. She looked happy and sad at the same time.

"I was hoping I'd run into you," she said as the door banged shut. "There's something I've been meaning to ask you about. There's a painting you have up on your bedroom wall there facing the window. I see it every time I take my laundry across the roof. That one there." She pointed. "Can I ask you who painted that?"

Well... I have to admit that she was actually pointing to one of my own artworks, a painting I had completed only a few months earlier of the birdlike creature with a human head that the Egyptians called the ba, the creature they believed represented a sort of soul. I had given it pride of place in my bedroom; at the time it was probably the one work I was most proud of. "That's one of mine," I said humbly.

"Really?" she replied, smiling broadly. "The ba?"

That surprised me. "You know it?" I asked, astonished.

She cocked her head to one side and stood up. "Let me show you something," she said, and turned back towards her apartment. After a moment, I stood up and followed her, feeling almost as though she was taking me by the hand.

Inside her apartment – along the floor, on tables, on stands and ledges – were dozens of papier-mâché sculptures rendered in blazing colour, ranging in size from tiny figurines to table-top dioramas, all of them depicting scenes from the mythology of Ancient Egypt. I was struck dumb, and she knew it; she watched me, smiling to herself, as I examined a sculpture of four baboons surrounding the Lake of Fire.

"This is..." I said to her, stupefied.

"Yes, yes, I know," she said excitedly. "I thought when I saw that painting of yours: really, not many people–"

"I know," I said. "I know."

We sat down at her kitchen table surrounded by her artwork and she made a pot of coffee and asked me about my paintings, and I told her about the current series I was working on. She asked me if I had seen a little papyrus-style birthday card depicting the Barque of Ra anywhere in the Peacocks' apartment; she had painted that for Rose for her seventieth birthday, she said. She had spotted the Hazlemere painting in the Peacocks' study when she was handing over her rent cheque one day and thought the sisters must be interested in Ancient Egypt. Actually, she said, laughing, they weren't particularly interested in Ancient Egypt at all; buying the Hazlemere had merely been one of many enviably far-sighted purchasing decisions they had made in the early 1960s.

"You painted that Barque of Ra?" I asked,

interrupting her.

"Yes," she said.

"It's wonderful," I said.

"Thank you," she said, and smiled.

She showed me a painting of the mutu, those poor souls so damned they were made to suffer a second death in the next world, and a palm-sized hollow scarab that an artist friend had made for her in which she kept all her loose change. I delightedly told her that I had for many years kept a very similar, although much smaller, jade scarab in my jeans pocket, in slightly whimsical accordance with the belief that carrying such a scarab would prevent your heart testifying against you on that dreadful day of judgment, that day of the weighing of the heart shown in the Peacocks' Hazlemere painting, when it was decided whether you would enter the afterlife or be consumed by the Devourer. But one day, not long after arriving in America, I forgot to take the scarab out of my pocket when I left my jeans at the laundromat and I never saw it again.

Who was she? She was a Portuguese girl who had come to New York as an art student, and, like everybody else, never left. She had always been interested in ancient mythology, she said – starting with the Lusitanians and moving on through the Romans, the Greeks, the Mayans and the Etruscans, before writing her final-year dissertation on Ancient Egyptian hieroglyphs and finding herself hooked, her own artwork – which at one point had been very derivative of Paula Rego – gradually becoming more and more influenced by the Egyptians'. Now she wrote about movies freelance for a fashion magazine by day and worked on her sculptures by night in a studio in Hell's Kitchen, and had been living in the small apartment adjoining the Peacocks' for nearly five years. She didn't mention her marriage, or her divorce – which was fine by me.

She told me fondly that her time at the Peacocks' had almost ended before it had begun when, soon after she had moved in, the sisters had had the small wall at the edge of the roof removed for restoration without telling her, and returning home from work that night and wandering to the edge of the roof to gaze out at the mesmerising lights of the city skyline she had almost toppled eleven storeys into the raging traffic of 77th Street. And she revealed that Rose had announced my arrival to her by pointing to my bedroom window, where they could both see me unpacking my things, and telling her feelingly, head cocked to one side: "Another lonelyheart." She told me the Peacocks viewed her apartment as being roughly the same, in privacy terms, as a daughter's bedroom: "Once I left them a voicemail asking if they'd mind giving me a bit of notice the next time they dropped round, and the next day when I got home there was a note on my bed saying they would be happy to." But she smiled affectionately as she recalled this; she seemed to like them anyway, warts and all.

I told her about my boss moving in on the fifth floor and she asked me to describe him and said, yes, she thought he was that middle-aged guy who'd said hi to her in the elevator recently – something I found made me hotly and unexpectedly furious. I told her about delivering the package to Marty Gamble's apartment, and she said that one time a parcel for her had been wrongly delivered to Marty Gamble's door, and Marty Gamble had brought it round for her and smiled and said, "I hope, whatever this is, that it gives you *great pleasure,*" and we laughed at that, but actually I was surprised to find that that made me pretty angry too.

We continued to talk. It got dark and we got hungry and we went downstairs to a bar on Madison and 76th and ordered some food and she asked me how well I knew the spells from the Ancient Egyptian 'Book of the Dead', and recited her favourite to me, delivering it with relish, leaning close over the tiny table as she did so: "O Rerek snake, take yourself off; Geb and Shu have arisen against you. For you have eaten a mouse, which Ra detests, and you have chewed the bones of a putrid cat."

That was one of my favourites too, and I replied with Anubis's spell for the mask: "Your right eye is the night boat. Your left eye is the day boat. Your eyebrows are the nine gods..."

She clapped when I finished, laughing. "I love that one," she said. I looked at her eyes, thinking of the night boat and the day boat; they were green but shot through with a burst of hazel like the Milky Way, her eyelashes long, black spikes.

I told her about the rare treat of being allowed into the study to drink champagne with the family, and about the banjos, and asked her if she'd seen all the other prints they had in there as well as the Hazlemere, the ones by Roy Lichtenstein and Alex Katz, for example.

"Oh, I don't think they're prints," she said. "Certainly when we talked about the Hazlemere they made it clear it was the real thing. Take a look at the brushstrokes on the aluminum paint he used for the heart when you get back."

"Wow, really," I said. "Well, I'll try. But they usually keep the study door locked."

"Just ask them if you can take a look."

"I bet they won't let me," I said. "You know what

they're like."

"Nick..." she said in that lugubrious tone that I would come to know well. "They are not your parents."

We left, passing a couple who seemed to be arguing because the boyfriend had been staring at Lydia's legs (I must admit I had snuck a couple of glimpses myself), and walked back to our building still happily telling Peacock stories, but once in the elevator a slightly pregnant silence fell. The front door to her apartment was beside mine in the hallway, and we stood outside the two doors saying nothing for a minute or two, and in the end she put out her hand and I shook it in what I hoped was a friendly fashion.

"Well," she said, "I had a lovely time. It's nice to get to know your neighbours."

"Maybe we can meet up and talk Egyptian relics some time," I said.

She smiled. "Yes," she said. "I'd like that."

*

Time passed. Young Annabel returned to Indonesia. The Peacock sisters returned to Long Island. I woke up one night to hear Frannie, their cat, scratching to be let out of the study – but I must have dreamt it;

41

they always took her back to Water Mill with them and would never have left her behind. After staying away from the city recovering from the excitement of Annabel's visit for a week or so, the sisters resumed their normal routine, and I resumed mine. I watered their plants with a glass of water and then sipped the rest myself. I flicked through their copies of the Wall Street Journal. I worked on paintings at my studio space in Bushwick and ate meals afterwards at the clangourous Chinese restaurant downstairs, where one night I was startled to receive a brisk text from Hannah reading, 'Hello Nick. The guy from my bank told me I have to confirm to you that all your payments have gone in now. I wish he didn't, but he did, so there you go, I've done it.' I sat there as the waiters shouted sharply to one another and hurried sizzling skillets across the room and I thought about that for a little while.

At work suddenly, presumably because of my new status as neighbour, I found myself invited to join friendly conversations with Samuel Latza whenever he would drop by, and my colleagues would stare at me, confused and jealous. But in truth he took me into his confidence no more than he did anyone else, being the kind of boss whose staff had to constantly scrape around to dig up the tiniest nuggets of information about their workplace. I remember once being in the storeroom stacking a new print carefully on a set of shallow shelves when I heard him talking to someone in the office next door.

"Jim... Campbell..." the other man was saying, perhaps writing the artist's name down. There was a pause. "So, what is it, it's made of light bulbs, this thing?"

"Yes," said Latza. "Red light bulbs. LED lights. They flicker on and off, and the – the voids created by the absence – the ones that are switched off – create the illusion that..." He tailed off.

"Right," said the other man. There was another pause. "And this was back in February?"

"That's right," said Latza.

"And when the other officers came by nobody asked you about the name Emilio Ruiz, or Emiliano Ruiz?"

"No," said Latza, his voice getting fainter as they left the office and moved out of earshot. "No, I don't think so."

One morning I was getting the elevator down to the ground floor when Marty Gamble blundered in, his eyes half-shut with tiredness, mumbling to someone on his cellphone.

"So what are you filming?" I could hear the tinny voice on the other end of the line ask him.

"Horror movie..." he replied. "Pretty low-budget."

"Sounds *terrifying*," the caller laughed.

At night, I would sometimes get a snack from the kitchen and glance at the reflections of Lydia's rooms in the plate-glass windows on the other side of 77th Street for a while with the light turned off. Once, in bed, from across the roof garden I heard a key turn in a lock and a muffled voice – was she with someone? Making a sketch at my desk of the goddess Ma'at for one of the headboards I was working on I found to my surprise that I seemed to be painting her: the dark darts of her eyelashes, the tiny lines either side of her half-open lips. I thought I had better change it in case she spotted what I was doing, and realised I was already thinking about the possibility of her visiting my room. Once I thought I saw her outside the Park restaurant near the High Line, but when she turned to cross the street it was somebody else.

Life with the Peacocks continued. I was getting used to it. A Wednesday evening might begin with Rose knocking on the bathroom door while I was in the bath, demanding: "Marie! Have you let the Carringtons know we're not coming?" and then chatting cheerfully to me through the door for fifteen minutes or so after discovering it was actually me in there. A Thursday morning might start with Marie accosting me on my way to work just as the elevator doors tried to shut and asking if I could quickly help her unload ten or eleven crates of wine from their SUV in the car park beneath the building, claiming; "It won't take a minute!"

Outside, on Madison Avenue, teenage girls from our building would stride across the street in high heels, legs locked in perfect time, while their younger brothers darted out of the entrance to the car park on bikes or scooters or skateboards and straight across Fifth Avenue, ducking self-importantly like the black gangstas they imagined they were so that no one could make out their faces, fleets of taxis stabbing like knives around them. I walked past the mouth of an alleyway on 77th Street every day, and every day the wind rustled up papers and plastic bags like a dog was down there, and every day I involuntarily quickened my pace in response.

One night, alone in the subway station, I heard a noise less high-pitched than usual, and turned to see a yellow goods train barrel along the tracks, its carriages half the height of a subway car, an utterly unexpected and confounding sight. Five seconds later, it was gone, and I found myself unable to completely banish the thought that I'd imagined the whole thing.

Sometimes I could hear it in the morning when Lydia would turn on the radio in her apartment to listen to the news.

*

One Thursday when I got home from work, Rose leapt up from her usual place at the kitchen table and offered me a cup of coffee.

"Thank you," I said, pleasantly surprised.

"Now, young Nicholas," she said in what she seemed to believe was a motherly fashion. "We have some friends coming over for dinner tonight, so if you're *going* to eat here... erm..."

"...do it now?" I asked.

"Exactly, dear, exactly," said Rose, beaming and pouring me my coffee. I had begun to find their trains of thought quite easy to follow. Basically, whatever was slightly outside the usual norms of politeness, that was what they were probably driving at.

So I was going out, it seemed. Rose returned to her paper, satisfied. Well, I thought rebelliously, I'm not going out just yet. I took my glasses out of my jacket pocket and picked up a section of her newspaper, and sat there next to her, reading. Just as I was finishing the arts reviews, I heard the familiar rustle of the laundry room door, followed by quick footsteps coming towards the kitchen.

"Miss Peacock?" Lydia called.

"In here, dear," Rose called back, not looking up. Lydia opened the door and came in, dressed in jeans and a loose blue T-shirt.

"I brought you the rent," she said, handing Rose a cheque.

"Why, thank you, dear," said Rose, folding it in two and putting it in a bowl on the table. "Always on time. I'll let Marie know it's there."

"Thank you," said Lydia. She turned to me. "Hello, Nick. Wow, are these your glasses?" I tried to take them off, but she moved towards me. "Let me see... Come here... Don't pretend you're not wearing glasses," she said, laughing, and Rose looked up quizzically from her paper, glancing quickly from one to the other of us.

"Hmm," she said, getting up. "Well, I'm going to leave you two to your young people's talk. Don't forget what I said about dinner, young Nicholas."

"Have they invited you to dinner?" Lydia asked when she'd left the room.

"No," I said. "The opposite. They've got friends coming round. I'm supposed to go out."

"Oh dear," she said. "Well, I suppose it *is* their apartment."

"It's my apartment too!" I said.

She gave me a sceptical look.

"Hey," I said. "You wouldn't happen to be – free tonight, would you? Do you fancy getting a bite to eat?"

"Only if you wear those glasses," she said.

"It's a deal," I said, smiling, and risked a slight joke: "Pick you up at eight?"

She laughed, and replied in kind, "Do you know how to find my place?"

"I'll borrow the Peacocks' GPS."

"Sure," she said. "Great. Eight it is."

She was on the phone when I knocked on her door, finishing off a call and sounding slightly annoyed. She had changed into a long, flowing wrap dress that looked like it was from the 70s – I suddenly realised I was staring at her and sat down sharply at the dinner table and examined an artwork in progress on the sideboard, a sculpture that showed a figure reaching its arms out towards its exact double. She switched her phone off with a sigh and put it in her handbag. "Is everything all right?" I asked.

"Oh, it's nothing," she said, sitting down. "The magazine I work for – they want me to write something for tomorrow morning. It's money, so that's great..." She smiled a bit. "But it's just that I was hoping to have a bit of time tomorrow to finish this sculpture."

"I'm sorry," I said, and rested my hand on her arm for a second.

"It's hard," she said. "I'm not exactly rolling in money here, so I feel like I can't turn any work down. I really want to get to the next stage with all this." She indicated the artworks all around us. "I'd like to put on a show. You know? I'd like to finish all these works, finish them properly and put on a show somewhere. I'd like to sell prints, get my name out there. But it all costs money. Money for prints, money for equipment, materials, money to rent the studio each week. And it's a vicious cycle, because every time the magazine offers me more work it just eats into the time I want to use for art. So I feel sort of – stuck. I need something like – what do Americans call it? – seed capital. Do you feel – do you feel like that?"

I thought about it. "I'm not sure," I said. "I'm not sure I'm at that stage yet. My pieces – I'm not sure there are enough there that I really feel are finished, not enough for a show, anyway."

"Oh, I'm sure there are," she said. "I'm sure there are. The ba?" she said, raising her eyebrows in a wordless compliment. "Well... you'll have to show me the rest."

49

*

She took me to a Portuguese fado restaurant near the Roosevelt Island tram stop. An elderly man sat hunched over a stool playing acoustic guitar as we ate, and a succession of female singers stood up one by one to accompany him for a few songs unamplified. Lydia translated the lyrics for me, but the only one that sticks in my mind now is the one that started: 'Never trust a man, because a man is the devil.'

We talked about Portugal. Her mother and father left school aged ten, she said. They had never wanted her to go on to college; they wanted her to go out and get a job as soon as she graduated. So she worked for two years answering phones and saving money and then with the help of one of her old teachers she won a scholarship to study fine art at NYU. She rarely went back home now. New York was home now. She watched the red cable car pensively climb the span of the Queensboro Bridge through the window. I told her that I was a foreigner too, that I came from a small-minded suburb on the threadbare fringes of south-east London, where the first thing I'd wanted to do was leave; leave my parents and my small-minded friends and neighbours and the roads that led nowhere and the streets that seemed to fall silent each evening as door slammed after door and the narcotic somnolent glow of the TV screens burned its way through net curtains and pebble-dash and plastic blinds. She raised her eyebrows a fraction when I finished that speech, which had ended up being rather longer and more colourful than I had intended, and I took my napkin off my lap and mumbled something unintelligible and went downstairs to the bathroom then, embarrassed at having strayed so far into hyperbole.

I said I'd heard her sometimes out on the roof garden talking in Portuguese. Oh yes, she said; probably talking to relatives, or to her friend Ana, a fellow Portuguese girl whom she had met here in New York. That was one thing she did miss over here, she said: the language. It was a beautiful language, Portuguese, she said, an expressive language, playful when it wanted to be, but (smiling now, making fun of my earlier speech) deep and dark like the black ocean, and heavy with the weight of its long history. Sometimes she still didn't know how to say exactly what she wanted to say in English, and she hated the feeling that she might be only half-expressing it. And she missed the imagery the Portuguese could call upon.

"We have so many amazing turns of phrase," she said: "'When a beggar receives...' Let me get it right...

'When a beggar receives lots of loose change, then he gets suspicious,'" she said.

I thought about it. "Is that something like '*do* look a gift horse in the mouth'?"

She laughed. "Sort of," she said. "I think it's closer to another one of yours: 'all that glitters is not gold'. But they're great, no? 'Fast and well, there's no one that can do it.'"

"'More haste, less speed,'" I said.

"'Whoever goes to the sea loses their place.' Now that's got to be better than 'you snooze, you lose.'" I laughed. "'Don't teach mass to the priest...'" she said.

I smiled. "'You can't teach Grandma how to suck eggs.'"

"Now that is one American saying I have never understood," she said. "Do grandmas suck eggs over here? Is that a thing?"

"I don't know," I said. "Maybe... maybe when the pioneers were heading west and they didn't have much to eat?"

She laughed. "One of my favourites," she said: "I think in English it's 'you might as well be hanged for a sheep as for a lamb.'"

"Yes," I said. "Or 'in for a penny, in for a pound'; that means the same thing. I think over here it might be 'in for a dime, in for a dollar'. So how do you say it in Portuguese?"

"'If you get into the water,'" she said softly, "'you might as well get wet.'"

*

We walked back to our building via the park. It was a lovely spring evening and we sat on the wall in front of the apartment block for a while as the sun set behind us. When she squinted against the light, little curving lines would appear at the edges of her eyes, like the way the Egyptians drew eyes. A strand of hair came loose from her hairband, and she tucked it behind her ear. Perhaps prompted by our earlier mention of grandmas, I told her about my old wooden Scrabble set, and asked her if she wanted to come up and have a game with me.

"I'd love to," she said, "but what about the Peacocks' guests?"

"Oh, yeah..." I said, remembering.

We took the lift upstairs and stood in front of our two front doors. "Why don't you go get the board and bring it round to mine?" she asked.

I brightened up. "Sure," I said. I slid quietly through the apartment and into my room. Voices and laughter were coming from the study, where the Peacock sisters always did their entertaining. I got the Scrabble board from the top of my wardrobe, and crept over to the Peacocks' wine rack by the study and picked out a bottle of red. But as I was examining the label the study door swung open with a burst of laughter, and, panicking, I slipped into the kitchen and raced quickly towards the shadows of the laundry room; the last thing I wanted was for them to see me on my way to Lydia's with a Scrabble board and a bottle of wine; I might as well have been holding a giant inflatable love heart. I gently eased open the laundry room door, tiptoed out across the roof garden, and knocked quietly on Lydia's door. From behind me there was a sudden noise, and I turned back in embarrassment to see Rose Peacock and a female friend of a similar age standing watching at the laundry room window. Rose raised her eyebrows enigmatically. I couldn't think how else to respond, so I waved.

Lydia and I played Scrabble and drank the bottle of wine, and then she taught me a Portuguese variation on the game, where you gradually removed the tiles, leaving whole words, until the board was completely bare. The metaphorical possibilities were endless.

While we played we continued to compare idioms. "How do you say 'add insult to injury'?" I asked her.

"Hmm..." She thought about it. "Well, I think

maybe we don't have that one."

"That's a great phrase," I said. "It's like if you set fire to someone's apartment, and then on the way out stole their favourite mug."

This unremarkable example was apparently hilarious. "'Favourite mug'?" she asked when she had stopped laughing. "Do you have a favourite mug, Nick? Do you all have a favourite mug back in England?" I laughed a bit too; I am quite prepared to laugh at myself if the situation warrants it.

"I guess the poor old chap couldn't have a cup of tea that night," she continued, with deep mock-compassion, before collapsing again into giggles. "I get the feeling adding insult to injury might be a particularly English thing to do," she added.

"Maybe you're right," I admitted.

"A bit like 'every cloud has a silver lining'," she said, shaking her head. "That really is not a Portuguese way of thinking."

I stayed as long as I could, but eventually she made it politely clear that it was time for me to go. I kissed her on the cheek to say goodbye and she kissed me on the other cheek, too, European-style, and then, on impulse, I gave her a hug, and we both laughed. Back at the Peacocks' the apartment was slumbering and the kitchen was a wreck; there would be a lot of work for Hyo-Sonn tomorrow. I poured myself a glass of wine from one of the half-drunk bottles the Peacocks and their guests had left on the table, and made my way back out on to the roof garden to drink it and smoke a cigarette. I sat on the little wall at the edge of the roof bundled up in my winter coat, the wine glass balanced beside me, listening to the howling streets far below and thinking about Lydia, the honk from a cab and the honk from a car horn combining fleetingly at one point to form a chord.

Through the midnight mist the skyscrapers were vague shapes, icebergs or Christmas trees. Her door was dark. Rain began to drum on the roof, and on my forehead and in my hair, and from somewhere nearby came the sudden keening of a police car.

Chapter 3

One evening, Marie phoned from Long Island. Lydia was out, and the Peacocks needed the measurements of the windows in her apartment. "Her blinds are always coming crashing down, poor dear. I promised her we would buy her some new ones." The spare key was in one of the drawers beside the stove, Marie said. The tape measure was in the laundry room.

I made my way across the roof garden and knocked on Lydia's door, and after a polite interval shouted: "Hello?" But she was definitely out. Quietly I slipped the key in the lock and opened the door. Her kitchen was silent, a couple of cups and a plate in the sink, potato chips going soft in a bowl on the coffee table. "Hello? Hello, Lydia?" I said to the empty air.

I quickly measured the kitchen window and noted down its dimensions. Next was the bedroom. I pushed open the door. Her large, ornate double bed had been left neatly made, which obscurely I

57

found somewhat disappointing. There were sculptures and paintings – many recognisable as her own – on the walls and shelves, and a series of black Egyptian cat figurines along her desk. By the mirror was a tastefully-constructed replica of Tutankhamun's torso, on which Lydia had hung some of her jewellery.

I walked over to the window and measured the frame. A few items of clothing were draped over the back of the chair beside the window, and I leafed through them: a black bra, a cardigan, a pair of jeans, and at the bottom of the pile the gauzy red tank-top she had been wearing when I had first seen her crossing the roof garden. It smelt of her.

Suddenly there was a noise from the kitchen or the roof garden and I gave a start, and stopped still, listening intently, wishing I had asked Marie when exactly Lydia was coming back. But after a moment or two's silence I decided it had probably just been a bird out on the roof, so I moved over to the other side of the room and opened the top drawer of her chest of drawers. There was nothing much in there – financial papers, art materials, photocopied flyers for an exhibition she had put on in 2006, an old, battered 35mm SLR camera, snapshots of her and a female friend trying on different hats in a photobooth somewhere – but in the second drawer, underneath a stack of envelopes, I came across a framed photograph that held my attention: Lydia with a Hispanic man, perhaps her ex-husband, perhaps the same guy I'd seen her with out on the roof that time, on holiday somewhere intimidatingly hot and sunny, Lydia looking incredibly attractive in a little blue bikini, the man's head strangely seeming slightly too small for his body – perhaps something to do with the angle of the picture. I held the photograph in my hands for a second or two, and then I put it back, closed the drawer, put the red tank-top in my back pocket, and left the apartment.

One evening a few nights later, I was upstairs reading in bed when I became conscious that the Peacock sisters were speaking quite sharply to one other in the kitchen. As I think I've said, the walls in the apartment were very flimsy, and it was usually easy to hear what was going on in other parts of the flat; nevertheless I put down my book and kept quite still so I could make out exactly what they were saying.

"An apartment block on Fifth Avenue is not a tenement in Queens," Rose said. "You're talking about almost every penny we have."

"Rose, do not exaggerate," said Marie. "It doesn't suit you. You have left these decisions to me before, and even if I do say so myself they have worked out extremely well for us. This one is going to be no different."

"Yes," said Rose. "But this – this is a very substantial proportion of our savings. It's the risk –"

"Rose, I'm sorry to say this, but when it comes to money I'm afraid you don't have the slightest understanding of the concept of risk. A risk was your suggestion that we should buy fourteen paintings by Alexandra Suskind for the economically-illiterate reason that they were 'only' one thousand dollars each and you 'liked' them! Alexandra Suskind now no longer troubles the art auctions of the world and I would be surprised if the one painting of hers that I did allow you to buy was now worth any more than a thousand *lire*!"

"Marie... That was a very long time ago."

"Indeed it was, which is why this example is now able to so precisely illustrate the limitations of your judgment. Alexandra Suskind was a risk. Her work might have become immensely valuable; it did not. Buying part of an apartment block on Fifth Avenue four or five blocks from here is not a risk – as long as one can afford the mortgage, which we can. Will there ever come a time when people do *not* wish to live on Fifth Avenue? Will there ever come a time when people will *not* pay vast sums of money to do so?"

"Maybe..." said Rose. "We don't know."

"Maybe," repeated Marie scornfully. "Yes, maybe... if the North Koreans detonate a nuclear bomb on 77th Street, in which case I don't think owning a hundred Alexandra Suskinds would protect us, or even a hundred Hazlemeres. Or if President Obama introduces a total amnesty for illegal immigrants, and Spanish Harlem suddenly expands all the way to the East Village – something I hope I will have been sensible enough to have seen coming and which will have prompted our own permanent exodus to Water Mill... or Canada. Rose," she continued decisively, "we will buy this share of the East Meadow Building, we will make vast sums of money in rent, and we will make even vaster sums of money when we eventually sell that share. Either that or we'll leave it to Austin and the children."

"But dealing with all those tenants, Marie... We've never taken on such a large number. And you've already said that these are a difficult set of people, many of whom have a history of vociferously opposing any sale–"

"That is *his* department!" Marie cried in exasperation. "Dealing with tenants is *his* department... And he's very good at it, as you know full well–"

"Marie, I may not know much about money, as you have so aggressively pointed out this evening, but I must say that I know a little bit more than you do about affairs of the heart, and I know that one of the reasons he continues to do business with us is in the hope..."

But they seemed to be moving into the living room, and I couldn't quite hear the end of the sentence.

"He does business with us because it's good business," Marie said firmly as they came back into earshot. "It's nothing to do with–"

"Marie, you simply do not have the slightest idea about these things," said Rose, her voice rising. "If I may go further, forgive me, you do not have the slightest idea about *men*. You've never been married. In fact, I'm not sure if a man has ever so much as looked at you. So perhaps you will listen to me on this particular subject. Right now he wants to work with us *primarily*, I am certain, in order to be close, in a limited sort of way, to her. But he may not feel that way for ever. What if he remarries and his new wife forbids it? What will we do then?"

"How dare you?" said Marie furiously, speaking over her. "You have no idea what I know or don't know about men. No idea. And I wouldn't say you're the world expert, in any regard – you certainly didn't know how to keep one!"

What I can only describe as a stunned silence followed that remark. I lay there motionless, keen to hear what was to come next. After a moment, Marie spoke again, in a placatory tone now:

"Rose... I apologise," she said.

"No," Rose replied brusquely. "No, no. You said what you thought. Thank you for your candour. As always. I really don't know what I would do without you. I think I shall go to bed now."

"Rose..."

"Good night, Marie."

There was another silence. I could hear Rose slowly climbing the stairs. "Good night," said Marie quietly from the living room.

*

A more senior job came up at work and Samuel Latza suggested I apply, and one evening a few days later I was working on my application when I heard Lydia coming in through the laundry room door. I got up from my desk and came out of my room, and we talked for a while as she held her basket of washing against her hip. We got on to the subject of our artwork, and she asked me if she could take a look at my painting of the ba; surprised and pleased, I led her into the apartment. The hallway lights took a few seconds to come on, and there was a moment when, although I had flicked the switch, we stood together in the darkness, and I was conscious suddenly of the heat of her body. Then the lights came on and we moved apart.

I watched her as she examined the paintings and photographs on my bedroom walls, and the sketches I had been working on at my desk.

"I remember the last lodger they had painted all the walls green," she said. "They were furious." She loved the ba, she said, standing in front of it, peering at the details of the wings. It was a beautiful piece of work. "Do you use the whole apartment, when they're away?" she asked me, perching lightly on my desk beside my sketchbook.

"Sure," I said. "I live like a king. Want me to show you round?"

"Are we allowed?" she asked.

"Lydia," I said sternly. "They are *not* our parents. In any case, they're away."

In the kitchen, she spotted the reflection of her own two rooms in the windows across the street, and asked me if I'd ever noticed that. No, I said. No, I hadn't. In the living room, she messed around on the piano with one hand, without sitting down, and lightly sang one of the songs from the fado club –

maybe the one about the devil. She was nervous about going upstairs to the floor where the sisters' bedrooms were – "What if they come back?" – but I talked her into it, and she enjoyed seeing her Barque of Ra birthday card framed beside Rose's bed, and was very intrigued by the little 'butler's room' crawlspace, which she had had no clue was there.

We sat down on the sofa in the library, pretending we were two students back in Rose's teaching days come to discuss our term papers with her. Facing us on the desk was a little model cat that looked like a phallus, and behind it a phallus that looked like a cat, and on the wall was a print of Georges Rochegrosse's almost unbearably sexual masterpiece 'Le Chevalier aux Fleurs', which shows the chaste and virginal knight Parsifal gazing angelically up to the heavens while a dozen naked, comely flower maidens gather around him on their knees and on their backs in the middle of a verdant meadow, their hands reaching seductively towards his legs and his waist and his bare neck, their fingers delicately caressing his gleaming armour. One of them gently rests her fingers on the tip of the handle of his sword. I'm not sure this painting would have quite put me at ease if I were a student here to visit my professor, but I suppose given Rose's field of study it successfully set the tone.

We leafed through some of the textbooks on the shelves, and I told Lydia that when I had first moved in to the apartment Rose had instructed me not to borrow any of her books, asking in bewilderment: "Why does everyone always want to borrow my books?" They were called things like: 'Sex: A Pictorial History', 'The Invention of the G-Spot' and 'Masturbation for Women: A Complete Guide to Taking Care of your Sexual Self'. Lydia laughed, and we sat back on the sofa flicking through 'What Men Really Want: Tips from a Pro', and when she spoke she inclined her body towards me, at first slightly, and then unambiguously. She was wearing a very tight, very thin white T-shirt, and my eyes ran over the shape of her body whenever she looked the other way. I wanted to touch her.

On the mantelpiece, she found a leaflet for a lecture series on depictions of the orgasm in twentieth-century cinema that Rose had hosted at Columbia in 1995. The FAQ for students on the back began with: 'Who can come?' We seemed to be laughing a lot. I was enjoying myself. But suddenly it was 1 a.m. and she said she had to go. I walked her to the laundry room door, where she spotted her washing in its basket on top of the washing machine, still unwashed, and we hugged goodnight on the step, and it felt different this time. It felt like she wanted to touch me too.

I closed the door behind me after she'd gone and poured myself a glass of white wine from an open bottle in the Peacocks' fridge, and sat down on the stairs in the hallway sipping the wine and replaying the events of the night in my mind. My hand brushed against something sharp on the stair and I looked down. It was a dead bee. I looked behind me, up the stairs: there were three or four on the steps to the Peacocks' part of the apartment; actually, five, six, seven... I put my drink down and gingerly climbed the stairs. As I searched for the light switch up there, something hard cracked under my shoe: the whole floor was littered with dead bees: the hallway, the bathroom, the Peacocks' bedrooms. In the butler's room, a live one crawled along a mattress, staggering forward almost drunkenly for a second before suddenly freezing stock-still like the last turn of a mechanical toy, making me shudder with disgust. I went into the kitchen, quite disturbed, got a dustpan and brush, and carefully swept them all up. But when I checked the next evening there were just as many again up there, or more.

Chapter 4

Without either of us really drawing attention to it, we gradually began to spend more and more of our time together. We would go for dinner, or go to the cinema, or sit together in her apartment and work on our art, and she began to appraise my pieces with a perceptiveness that I realised I had sorely needed.

I loved watching her work. I admired her pride in her own pieces, her perfectionism and attention to detail, the way she would peer down through a magnifying glass for minutes to examine some tiny detail, the way she was always willing to rip everything up and start again if it would improve one small aspect. I loved the skill and originality of her work, and I began to feel as proud of it as I was of my own. We would talk about the day we would be able to jack it all in and devote our working lives full-time to our artwork, joking about the shabtis who did the work of their owners in the Land of the Dead. (In some respects the Ancient Egyptians had it easy.) In the real Egypt during those weeks, people were out on the streets trying to topple their dictator and then their army, but we weren't interested in that; we were interested in the ba and the ka, in the heart speaking up against you and the second death and the Barque of Ra. We did not introduce each other to our friends. There were no family members to be negotiated. It felt like we were starting again from scratch. It felt like it was year zero. And to be honest, I was glad to reinvent myself; glad to slough off my former, slightly unsatisfactory life like a snake's old skin, happy to be reborn. In many ways this was the life I had always wanted: two artists, alone. It felt like I had been looking for something, and I had found it.

Except that at the end of each evening we would part with a platonic hug and I would return reluctantly to the Peacocks' apartment, alone.

We went to a press screening of a movie set on our block, and Samuel Latza was in the movie theatre too, and I was proud to be seen with Lydia, glad to be seen with her, and I stopped to talk as we walked past him so he could see us together. Hyo-Sonn accidentally vacuumed up one of Lydia's diamond ear-rings and I cut open the dust-bag to try to find it, and found it. It was a beautiful ear-ring, I told her, before asking who had given them to her. And she replied quietly: "Hector."

I caught Marty Gamble drooling over her in the lobby of our building when she was wearing a short skirt that showed off her beautiful brown legs. A passing police helicopter shook our wine glasses when we were outside on the flat roof drinking a bottle of wine, and rattled the glass in the windows. We passed a bar where, she told me, she used to work as a student, and I caught a glimpse of a barmaid in a revealing outfit as a group of young men came crashing out through the front door. We tried to go to a Mediterranean restaurant around the corner from our building, but the maître d' said: "I'm very sorry, sir, miss, but we only have this one table free, and Mr..." – reading the handwritten card between the cutlery – "...Mr 'Marty Gamble' has booked it from 9 p.m."

Ai Weiwei's Sunflower Seeds came to town, one hundred million tiny porcelain replica sunflower seeds in a huge pile at the Mary Boone Gallery, and when Lydia was looking the other way I bent down to tie my shoelace and pocketed one of the seeds, and when we arrived back home at our two front doors I opened my palm and presented it to her and she looked up at me, shocked and delighted. She was wearing a soft blue trench coat and matching hat, and she looked like the star of a film noir, and the cab drivers wondered who we were, this young couple, this elegant beautiful young woman being swept home to the rich upper reaches of the Upper East Side. We went for dinner that night, and a couple began to argue because the girl had caught the guy looking at Lydia as we were leaving, and I felt proud that she was mine, and then I remembered with a painful wrench that she wasn't, she wasn't at all, and I suddenly felt sick and nervous, nervous that in fact somebody else could be sleeping with her and I wouldn't even know. This guy, this lech staring at her right now, *he* could be sleeping with her, for all I knew; maybe that was why he was staring at her: he was wondering who the hell I was, he was wondering why Lydia was ignoring him... I remembered that muffled voice I had heard from her apartment soon after I had moved in, the key turning in the lock. Who had that been? Perhaps just her friend – perhaps just her friend Ana, or another friend, a female friend. But I was sure it hadn't been a woman's voice.

A few days later when I came home from work I noticed a man standing on the corner of Fifth Avenue and 77th Street, staring up at the top floor of our building, at what must have been Lydia's windows. The windows stared back at him, black and blank. I followed his gaze; there was a hint of slight activity up there and he started forward on one

71

foot, but it was nothing, just the reflection of a plane going past, and he stepped back again into his original position. As I stumbled through the front doors and into the lobby, rather disconcerted, I glanced back and saw clearly that he was now staring at me, intense eyes rocking in a head that seemed slightly too small for his body. The setting sun glinted off something on his left hand that might have been a wedding ring.

She told me about her divorce, awkwardly, slowly. "They were quite close, Hector and the Peacock sisters," she said. "He helped them buy some property out in Queens about five years ago – that was how we met them – and then he set up property deals for them from time to time over the next few years. They were very upset when he moved out – especially Marie, I think. She's the business brain of the two of them, as I'm sure you've noticed."

Slightly nervously, I asked her why they had split up.

"It just–" she said. "It just ended. We're still – we meet up from time to time. We're still on good terms. He spends a lot of time out of the city. I see him when he's here, sometimes. I do try to see him." She trailed off. "What about you, and... Hannah?" she asked. I told her it ended amicably, and to change the subject pointed to the portrait of Queen

Nefertiti framed in imposing style on the wall across from her bed, her face almost fully silhouetted by the disk of the blazing red sun that she worshipped, rays of crimson light arcing out in all directions, one of Lydia's most impressive pieces. When had she painted it? Six years ago, she said after a while, stirring her coffee meditatively, not looking at me. It had been a present to Hector on their wedding day. I watched her watching her coffee as it swirled sadly in a circle. She suddenly felt quite distant.

Having noticed me often outside chatting to Lydia on the flat roof, the Peacocks had taken to asking after her when they saw me, and Marie did so again when I got home from work that night.

"Lovely girl," she mused, and I nodded inscrutably. "Smart girl, very clever. One day she'll sell all that damn strange artwork of hers and make her fortune!" I smiled. "Shame about Hector," she continued regretfully. "Very sad. Friendly young man, very bright. Great nose for business... That's how we first met the two of them, as I'm sure you know. He helped us strike a few property deals over in Queens some years ago. Very satisfactory for all concerned, I think. A few months after that first deal he told us he and his wife wanted to move into the city; we said we had the perfect place and they moved into the apartment right here." She gestured briefly in the direction of Lydia's door. "What a shame..." she concluded unexpectedly with a sigh, obviously remembering some detail of their break-up.

"What happened?" I asked, perhaps less inscrutably now.

"What happened? I don't know, dear," Marie said frankly. "Neither of them ever explained it to us, and naturally we never asked. Hector just came over here one night, very properly, that respect for formalities the Spanish – I mean the Hispanics – still have, and explained that he was moving out, very humbly asked if we would consider reducing Lydia's rent, since she would be living there on her own from now on. Well, of course we said yes. We still do business with him, of course, poor thing, but in some ways he's never really been the same since. I'm not sure she has either, to be perfectly honest." She seemed lost in thought. "Very sad indeed," she concluded.

Around the same time I got an email from Severin saying that Rose Peacock had asked her if anything was 'going on' between young Nicholas and young Lydia – 'because he seems to be spending a lot of time at her apartment, and once, late at night, I heard them listening to jazz – and people only listen to jazz late at night for one reason!'

I told Severin that nothing was happening; I had

just been over to borrow a lightbulb.

"And the jazz...?" Severin asked.

"Lots of people listen to jazz," I said firmly. "Nothing is happening. If they ask you about it again, can you please misdirect them..."

"'Misdirect them'?" she repeated delightedly, and a few days later she contacted me again. She and Jeff had just been up to Water Mill for a family gathering at Jeff's parents'.

"So we were all in the hot tub..." she began.

"Who was?" I asked, a bit thrown by this exotic opening line.

"Well, me, Jeff, his mom, his dad, his aunts, a couple of the Peacock cousins."

"Wow," I said. "Cosy."

"The Peahens, I call them," she went on. "They're like, seventeen-year-old girls. Jeff doesn't know where to look. They're like his cousins, you know... Anyway, and then Rose asks, 'So what's happening with young Nicholas's love life? We never see any girls coming or going.'"

"Right," I said apprehensively. "So what did you say?"

"Don't worry, I misdirected them," she said. "I said: 'I *think* young Nicholas is a homosexual...'"

I groaned.

"But Marie rushed to your defence. She said to

everyone: 'Young Nicholas is *not* a homosexual.' She said: 'Young Nicolas spends his time puzzling over ageless artistic quandaries, ruminating on his formative years in a Europe sunk deep in moral decline, and studying the mythology and symbology of Ancient Egypt. He's an ascetic. He has no time for women.'"

"Wow," I said.

"Yeah, but wait wait wait. And then Rose said wistfully, 'You know, it's such a shame young Annabel is spoken for. They really seemed to hit it off when she came home last time.'"

"Wow," I said again.

"Maybe *your* last name will be Peacock soon," Severin concluded innocently.

*

That night I dreamt about the Devourer. I was in the Hall of Judgment, in the middle of the scene Edward Hazlemere had depicted so vividly in the painting on the Peacocks' study wall, my ba flitting nervously around my head, waiting while Anubis adjusted the scale weighing my heart against the feather, his black jackal's head gleaming lasciviously, his red eyes flickering. Thoth stood writing with his long reed brush, a priestly white sash across his chest. I noticed gods lined up above us, seated and stern, and could sense somewhere invisible the presence of Osiris, the king of the dead, before my attention was called back to the scene before me: the Devourer shuffling slowly across the floor, its hippopotamine hindquarters lumbering awkwardly and out of step behind those restless lion's front legs. I tried to concentrate on what Anubis was doing, but I couldn't take my eyes off the Devourer, that crocodile's head, those deep-set green eyes that looked as though they had been on the planet since animals first dared crawl out of the sea, the harsh folds of its scaly skin, the teeth longer than the height of its snout, jutting like daggers, glistening in the pitiless sunlight. As I watched, it opened its jaws and I caught a glimpse of a yellow tongue, rotten and foamy. I slapped my pockets anxiously, looking for my scarab so I could prevent my heart speaking up against me, before remembering I had lost it in the laundromat years before. Anubis let go of the scales, and my heart and the feather beside it sank and swayed, up and down, as they began to find their level. My ba murmured worriedly at my ear, and my heart began to dip lower...

And then I woke up, a breeze from a chink in the window-frame ruffling my hair like a hand.

*

That Friday I took her to the American Society of Photographers private view at the Bialystoker synagogue on the Lower East Side.

"We're with the – with the – you know," I told the doorman, pointing vaguely towards a conclave of essential-looking guests as we wove our way through the busy crowd thronging the entrance. We asked for two glasses of white wine from the free bar. Lydia was gazing around at the building's luminescent stained glass windows.

"It's beautiful," she said.

"Are you two on the list?" asked the waitress.

"We certainly should be," I replied ambiguously.

She looked at us, and for some reason relented. "Well, I didn't serve you," she said, passing us our drinks.

"And I didn't tip you," I replied, handing her a note, and Lydia smiled.

We wandered over to the walls to look at the photos; they were news and celebrity shots mostly, but Lydia honed in on unusually-framed picture of a group of swans – a lamentation of swans, I believe is the proper term.

"They're like the supermodels of birds, aren't they, swans?" she said.

At around midnight, the show began to close down; we looked at a photo of a stripper next to a French couple. "Stripping's always so boring," said Lydia. "They need to mix it up a little. It's always the same: shirt, you know, bra. I would do it, like, from out of a straitjacket." The French couple began to giggle.

"You really should," said the Frenchman.

I ducked out for a second and came back with a print of the swans. "A present," I said to Lydia.

"No..." she said. "It's lovely, but... oh, Nick, was it very expensive?"

"Not really," I replied, which was true. I found a plastic portfolio case under one of the rows of pews, if that's what they're called in a synagogue, and packed the print away for her.

"Well, thank you," she said feelingly.

"Are you coming to the after-party?" the Frenchman asked.

"The after-party..." said Lydia. "Where was that again?"

"I have a flyer," said the French girl, and we fell into step with the crowd as they migrated slowly up towards Alphabet City. In the club, we checked the print of the swans into the cloakroom and danced, pushed close together by the crowd, the bassline of the music rataplanning off the walls. Lydia was wearing a short black dress with a crisp white collar, and she held the hem of the dress between her fingers and thumbs and swished it back and forth as she danced forward and back. The room seemed to revolve around her. I couldn't take my eyes off her. Her white sunglasses were pushed back up into her spiralling hair and I could see my face reflected in the lenses. The Frenchman's girlfriend had disappeared and he was now trying to talk to Lydia.

"Are you an artist, or photographer? Or a model? Do I recognise you?" he asked her, spilling champagne on my shoes as he lurched towards her.

"No, no," she said. "We work in insurance, uptown. Very boring." And then she danced out of his reach and next to me, and lightly took hold of my hand, and I span her and turned her like the dancers of the 1940s.

And it's strange, looking back now, how even after so long I can remember so clearly all these incidents and dreams and nightmares and scraps of conversation – or maybe I can't, maybe I'm just covering over the gaps between memories like a blanket pulled tight, warm and reassuring across a bed. It always seemed to be night in those early days, always seemed to be dark. I always seemed to be dreaming. Streetlights orange at the windows. The rumble of the subway underfoot, the engines hitting the first note of 'Rhapsody in Blue' as they started up. Crimson sunsets settling on the walls of the skyscrapers to the south. Police sirens approaching, flailing wildly like dervishes, and then disappearing, sliding past and away. They didn't get you this time.

*

Lydia had to go upstate to a small town called Horseheads, NY, to interview a film director for her magazine, and I offered to drive her up there.

"Do you have a car?" she asked.

I didn't, but I knew where the Peacock sisters kept the key to theirs: in a wooden box shaped like a bear's paw in the living room, along with a number of sewing-related items and another key, this one huge and cartoon-like, that I assumed was probably for the study.

"They never use that Toyota anyway," I said. "They always go back and forth to Water Mill in the SUV. We'll fill the tank back up, put it back exactly where it was as soon as we get back. They'll never even know we touched it."

"I don't know..." she said doubtfully.

"It'll be fine," I said. "Jeff borrows it all the time."

"Does he?" she said. "But they've probably told him he can do that. Have they ever said you could borrow it?"

"Well, not specifically," I said, "but, you know, it's all part of the apartment, really, isn't it? When I moved in, you know, they specified all the things they didn't want me to use – their fridge, their telephone – and I think the assumption was that everything else was mine to use."

She smiled, raising an eyebrow. "Was it? Was that the deal?"

I laughed. "Well, it's not really a normal rental arrangement here, is it? They expect me to keep an eye on the whole apartment for them whenever they're away; I bet that would include the car. And in return, they know I'll use everything in here."

"I just don't think a *car* is part of an *apartment*," Lydia said.

"Lydia..." I said. "The Peacocks have got so many cars. They've got two here; they've probably got another two in Water Mill. And this one is just sitting there doing nothing, when we really need one so we can go up to Horseheads. It's a waste that it's just sitting there, when it would really help us out just to borrow it."

She smiled. "You're very persuasive," she said.

I smiled too.

"It'll be great," I said. "We'll have a great time. A long drive upstate, sunroof open in the sunshine." I was sure it had a sunroof. "The open road. This is what America's all about. We've never driven anywhere together before, the two of us. We'll have a great time."

"Well..." she said. "It does sound like it would be fun."

"It'll be great fun," I said. "We'll have a great time."

"Okay," she said, shaking her head and smiling. "Okay."

Chapter 5

We met in the hallway outside our two front doors early that Saturday morning, overnight bags in hand, feeling – in my case anyway – as though we were running away from home. The car park in the basement was enormous and there were three or four very similar Toyotas parked down there, but luckily the first one I tried turned out to be the Peacocks' and we threw our bags in the trunk and clambered in. The doorman gave us a friendly wave as we drove out into the early-morning glare, and I put my sunglasses on with a flourish. It felt wonderful to have Lydia beside me in the passenger seat. Surely tonight...

We crept up Madison Avenue under the cool black shadows of the shops, followed the route of the Harlem River, and were soon out above the Hudson on the high wire of the George Washington Bridge, heading into New Jersey, the little red lighthouse in Fort Washington Park blazing away determinedly below us, the ancient, unspoilt foliage of the river's west bank spread out before us as if we were driving back into the past.

She was talking about her parents. She used to go home once a year, she said, usually at Christmas. One year she skipped it – finishing a sculpture for a January art fair – and to her surprise found that she didn't really miss any of it at all: the painful efforts to rewind her personality, interests and beliefs back to the moment when they had frozen in her parents' minds, probably somewhere around age twenty, the increasingly distant relatives and diminishing band of friends, the awkward attempts to bridge the distance between lives that were unstoppably and irreversibly floating away from one another like continental plates. So after that it became once every two years, and now it was getting on for four since she'd seen them last.

"Do they ever come out here?" I asked.

"No," she said, turning to watch the indomitable wall of buildings shrink rheumily behind us. She was wearing thin black leggings tucked into long tan boots. "I'd love them to come. I'd love them to see where I live. I'd love to show them who I am over here. I'd love them to understand all that. But they would never come. They've never been on a plane, you know. They've never left Portugal. Maybe day-trips to Spain."

"Yes," I said.

"And you?" she said after a little while. "Do you go back to England much?"

I warily negotiated the complicated off-ramp for the I-95. "I went back once," I said. "A year or so into college. It wasn't... It wasn't a success. You know, when I first got here I felt so British. The way I talked, the way I thought. People told me that all the time. But by the time I went back for that visit I think I had become American through and through. And I just felt that I had no interest at all in that strange, cold little island, you know, out there in the middle of nowhere."

"And your parents?" she asked. "Do they come visit?"

"You know..." I told her. "I really haven't... I don't speak to my parents very often. You know. There were many... aspects of our relationship where we didn't get on very well, and after I moved out here it just seemed, more or less, like it was time to, you know..." I trailed off. It had been hard to explain this to Hannah too. "So I just don't... We speak on the phone sometimes. I haven't seen them in a long while," I said finally. "So I guess you and I are in the same boat, so to speak."

She didn't say anything. She was watching the road again. "The only time it hurt..." she said. "You know, they couldn't come to the wedding ceremony. We got married here in New York," she said, slightly haltingly. "In Queens. They couldn't afford to come. We got married here, with his family, with our friends here – he's American; his parents came over from Portugal in the 60s – and then we flew over to Lisbon and we had a family party with my family there; my family, a few of his older relatives: his grandparents."

They got married a year after they met, she said. She had felt young, at twenty-six, but he was older, and he seemed so sure and ready, and that made her feel sure too. With him she suddenly felt like an adult, she told me, and if two adults wanted to get married, well, that was what adults did. Her mother and father showed no surprise when she told them. She put them on speakerphone and introduced them to him and they immediately started asking him about kids. She could imagine her mother's face. She could picture her mother's pupils practically turning into rattles as she spoke.

Lydia had loved the wedding. There had been such an atmosphere of happiness; everyone had seemed so pleased; they were all there to celebrate this incontestably good thing, their relationship, their happiness. And she felt happy in some deep and fundamental and probably un-PC way to be marrying into another Portuguese family – or perhaps happy is not the word: content, or complete, or something... it felt right somehow, it felt comforting to think that here, five thousand kilometres away from home, or three thousand miles, as she was starting to think of it now, she would still have a version of that culture and identity around her. Portugal had held her back, she felt, but it was her, it was part of her. And when she woke up that morning she felt ready. It was *right.* She wanted their lives to join together. She felt so close to him. They were two points on a line, looking at each other along the line. The car crept towards the church. It was hard to get in and out the door, what with the dress; it took up so much space that later on it was difficult for people to get near enough to dance with her. It had been made by a fashion-designer friend of hers from art school; he'd also designed the long purple dresses worn by the bridesmaids: her friends Katy and Ana, Hector's sister Celia and his young cousin Teresa. They worried about her dress, the bridesmaids, worried she was going to catch it on something. They worried about her tiara slipping loose. But Lydia didn't worry. She felt it was going to be all right. She saw her friends to her left as she walked into the chapel, turned to the right and saw Hector's family, Hector's friends. She couldn't stop beaming. She gripped the arm of Hector's father, who her own father had insisted by letter be the one to give her away since he would not be able to, and she held her bouquet bolt upright. And there was Hector, at the front of the church, at the altar. He seemed very nervous, fumbled a little when he was putting on the ring, messed up his lines a little bit. He kept looking at her and giving her little excited smiles. He held her hand tightly throughout. But as soon as it was all done he seemed to relax and he hugged her and whispered, "I'm really happy."

"So am I," she replied.

"I was really nervous," he said.

"Why?"

"I don't know," he said. "It's so important to get it right. I didn't want to mess anything up."

"You didn't mess anything up. Don't worry. You were great," she said, and she kissed him on the cheek.

They walked out to the front of the church for photos and Hector gripped her hand proudly. They beamed into the cameras and held each other's waists. Their guests, their friends, his family, began to sweep around them, sipping champagne or orange juice and waiting almost politely, she thought, to congratulate her and give her a kiss. More photos in the garden. It was a beautiful spring day, the sky dotted with tiny, high-up white clouds.

They had the wedding reception at a cavernous restaurant in Astoria belonging to Hector's uncle. She danced with Hector and he had to get his feet under the wedding dress before the song started to keep himself from treading on it. She crossed her hands around his neck. She leant her head on his shoulder. People were chatting in corners all over the restaurant. A waiter poured her another glass of champagne and she chatted with Hector's sister Celia. She looked gorgeous in her bridesmaid's dress, her hair twisted and set in complicated patterns. Somebody took her away to dance. Ana materialised from the crowd and gave Lydia a hug.

"Parabéns," she said, kissing Lydia on both cheeks. Congratulations.

"Obrigada," said Lydia, and she held Ana tight for a second. She felt Ana understood what she was feeling – all the complicated emotions she was feeling. Ana was an exile too.

At the hotel that night she lay across Hector's lap on the bed as he laboriously untied her wedding dress. "That was a tiring day," she said happily.

"Oh yeah," he said. "Whew."

"Drunken day," she said. They laughed. "Good, though." She reached out for his hand.

"It's been really good," he said.

"Everybody looked so nice."

"They did."

"All dressed up so smartly."

"You looked amazing. You *look* amazing."

"Thank you..." she said. "I can't wait to see Florida."

"You'll love it."

"Did you order a cab?"

"It's coming at nine."

They had met through her uncle. Her uncle and Hector's parents had gone to school together, decades ago, back in the old country, and when she moved to New York her parents had insisted she look them up. She didn't for a while. She didn't really know them and the seemingly inexhaustible excitement of New York was taking up all her attention and all her free time. But in the end, her parents gave the Soareses her number instead and they called her, and at that point she knew she couldn't say no. The first time she went across to Jackson Heights for dinner it was just the three of them. But the second time they invited their son.

Hector called her up a few days later and asked her if he could take her to the top of the Empire State Building. I know you'll think it was a cliché, she told me. It was cliché. But because it was so cliché she'd never actually been up there before. And it was thrilling to see how it all fitted together: the streets and the grid, the rivers and the park. The enormous country was spread out behind her and New York was leading it like the prow of a ship. Her lips were chapped and sticky in the cold air; the wind caught her hair as she leant her head through the barriers. Down there, in the X of Broadway and Fifth, the cabs were roaring off their marks when the lights turned green and switching lanes with terrifying abandon. Hector was wearing a baseball cap low over his face and watching her as much as he was watching the streets. The decaying warehouses of Queens and Brooklyn. The Chrysler Building delicate and gleaming like a champagne flute. The ragged silhouette of the buildings in front of the park, windows sparkling, plate glass reflecting the wintry blue sky, the sheets of offices hanging high above the rushing streets. The fire escapes clinging on to whole blocks for dear life. The empty space where the towers of the World Trade Center should have been. It was still not long since they had come down, and she felt suddenly that they were both remembering them then, those huge grey slabs peeking over the rooves and water towers, as if the roads had suddenly taken a ninety-degree turn and decided to flow straight up.

"You know my mother still won't fly," said

Hector.

"She won't?"

"No, like – I had to get a plane to Philly on September – nineteenth, I think it was, and I mean I'm not a panicky person – 2001, this is – but even I, I just froze up," he said. "I couldn't do it."

"No way," she said.

"For days you didn't see a plane in the sky," recalled Hector. She remembered it herself. It had felt as though America had come to a standstill. Like it was frozen to the spot in shock.

She tracked the progress of a car down Fifth, looking deep into the wells of the city streets. It was a small city, in size. But it packed so much in. Her gaze travelled out into the bay, to the Statue of Liberty.

"I had an idea for a joke," she told him. "But I couldn't think of a punchline."

"How does it start?" asked Hector.

"It starts: Statue of Liberty walks into a bar."

"Hmm," said Hector. He gazed out over the rooftops and the water towers, thinking. "Okay, no, wait–" he said. "Something about it's green... green around the gills...?"

"It's hard, isn't it?"

"It seems like it would be so easy... Something about the torch...?"

"Maybe he thinks she's trying to bring her own drink in..."

"Open container... Yeah... I don't know. Hold on, I'll think."

She suggested the restaurant, a place over in Dumbo tiled like an old public swimming pool, dark and monochrome, mirrors and round tables. It was cramped; she and Hector were knee-to-knee, and whenever she pulled back her hand to cut her pork chops she almost bashed another diner in the back. But the other diner was oblivious. "What the fuck do they care?" he was saying to his companion. "Over in Sicily?"

She watched Hector eating, and he saw her watching. "I like those lines you get, by your eyes, when you're concentrating," she said. He leant over and kissed her on the cheek, and she moved away slightly, not quite ready to accept, not yet, and smiled and said: "I hope you're thinking about the Statue of Liberty."

"I tell you what I'm thinking. I'm thinking: if I ask for another side is she gonna think: 'This is the greediest man on planet earth and I'm never gonna go out with him again for as long as I live,'" said Hector. She laughed.

They waited in the doorway of the restaurant for a long time for a cab, and it was cold. "Now I know why they call it Dumbo," said Hector genially; "it's because you'd have to be a fucking idiot to live here." They both laughed. They couldn't hear themselves over the noise of the trains thundering across the bridge above them.

"That is one noisy bridge," said Lydia.

The taxi took them back to her apartment – she was living on the Lower East Side then – and Hector asked her, very politely, if she might want some company, and she said no, that time, but the next week, after she had spent the whole evening talking to him about the new artwork she had just started, a painting of the sky goddess Nut stretched out across the horizon, blending into the sunset above the desert, he had responded with such enthusiasm that she had wanted to show him what she'd done so far, wanted to know what he thought of the real thing, wanted to know what he thought of her artwork, what he thought of her as an artist, not just as a pretty girl, or a charming girl, or whatever it was that had first attracted him to her, so she let him come up to her studio apartment, where canvasses were piled against canvasses by the walls and doors, under the windows, beside the bed, which she deliberately hadn't made because she had promised herself before going out that evening that she wasn't going to let him come up, and which she now quickly threw the bedspread across as they entered the room. He sat down on it as soon as the bedspread was down, so to divert him she suggested they go up to the roof for a cigarette.

"What about the painting?" he said.

"We'll look at it when we come back down."

The Williamsburg Bridge rose up beside them as their breath froze in the night air.

"It's quieter than the other one," said Hector, watching the cars.

Faintly, from the apartment below, they could hear the bass and vocals of a Stevie Wonder song, and Hector softly moved towards her, and held her at her waist, and they began to dance. She dropped her cigarette. He was quite a good dancer. Relaxed. She wondered if it came with age.

"I'm glad I met you," she said, almost without realising it.

"Me too," he said softly, and she suddenly became nervous.

"I love this neighbourhood," she said, looking out over his shoulder at the crosswalks and awnings of the streets below. "At art school I took some credits in video installation and I had this idea for a Martin Scorsese version of 'The Stone Raft', I don't know if you know Saramago's 'The Stone Raft', where Little Italy and the Lower East Side would break off from the rest of Manhattan and start floating away into Upper New York Bay, and you'd change the character of the dog to make him a pimp or a drug dealer wracked with doubts about his Catholic faith. I mean the Catholic stuff just reads straight across... What do you think?"

He laughed. "I think it's great," he said. And she kissed his shoulder through his shirt.

It was sunny and warm when she woke up next to him, her paintings stacked beside the bed, but out on the streets under the shadows of the buildings it was cold as they walked around the block to get breakfast, as if it were only sunny above a certain floor. Lydia put on an extra sweater under her coat, and even Hector, who normally seemed happy in a T-shirt whatever the weather, pulled his jacket around himself more tightly than usual.

"If it's burnt, I'm gonna send it back," an old lady was saying to the counterman as they bundled into an Italian diner. "What am I gonna do, eat it?"

They waited for their breakfast, facing each other across the booth, both keeping pretty quiet. She wasn't sure what he was thinking. She was thinking about him. She was thinking about last night.

"Do you feel at home here, in New York, now?" he asked her.

"I don't," she said after a little while. "And I don't

feel at home at home, either." She smiled, but he didn't smile.

"I don't want you to feel that way," he said. "I want you to feel at home."

They were quiet, and then he smiled and shook his head. "Statue of Liberty walks into a bar," he mused. "It's a great image..."

*

We stopped for petrol just outside of Ho-Ho-Kus.

"I'll pay," said Lydia, stopping me reaching for my wallet. "We're only taking this trip because of me." She counted out some notes, and then pulled that scarab full of change she'd shown me at her apartment out of her bag.

"Do you take that everywhere you go?" I asked, looking at the scarab.

She looked bashful. "Not everywhere," she said. "I just – I thought you might like to see it." It gleamed red and gold as the sunlight struck it through the windshield.

"It's beautiful," I said. "I wish I still had mine."

"To be honest, I'm a bit superstitious about it," she said. "You know, I was thinking about that Hazlemere painting the Peacocks have up in their study – 'The Weighing of the Heart.' I found that whole concept so fascinating when I first read about it, in college, that whole idea that your own heart could speak out against you on the Day of Judgment, and you'd need a little heart scarab like this to stop it doing so."

"Yes," I said.

"It's such a strange thought, isn't it, that your own heart would testify against you, that you couldn't trust your own heart to be on your side. You would be standing up there in the Hall of Judgment somewhere deep in the underworld of Osiris, in front of Anubis, in front of Thoth, in front of the Devourer, and it would be revealing all your secrets. And who'd know your secrets better than your own heart, you know?"

"Yes," I said.

"It makes me shiver to think about it," she continued, almost delightedly. "You know, some of the spells even begged the heart not to tell *lies* about its owner. You know, telling secrets is bad enough, but outright *lies*? Wow. That's another matter." She shook her head, smiling. "And there's Thoth, and there's Anubis, and behind them there's the Devourer, sitting there waiting, listening to every word – and if your heart is too heavy, if your heart pushes down the scale..."

I glanced across at her; she seemed to be looking

out and ahead along the highway, but I could see
what she was really seeing, I knew what she was really
seeing: the Devourer, feasting on the damned, slicing
into them with sharpened knives, sinking its dark,
dreadful teeth into their necks. We set off again and
swept down a long, elliptical hill, sheep scattered
across the landscape like scraps of paper.

In Horseheads, I waited in the car while she
interviewed the director in the front room of his low-
slung one-storey house. It was a bleary, broiling
town, the horizon swallowed up by dust and heat-
haze, the buildings squat and unremarkable.
Nobody passed by the car the whole two hours I was
sitting there. The sun crept gradually across the sky
behind me, dazzling in the rear-view mirror, and the
sweat swept down my forehead in surging swells. I
could see the two of them through the window of
the house. I messed around with the radio, flicked
the driver's mirror up and down a couple of times,
thought about the hotel I'd booked us for that night,
thought for quite a long time about what she'd told
me about Hector and their wedding and how they
had met, went on watching her and the director.

The director was in his late sixties, with long grey
hair and a grizzled jawline. He stared intensely at
Lydia as they spoke, and I caught occasional glimpses
of rows of tiny, black-looking teeth. Their

100

conversation seemed quite animated, but Lydia wasn't taking any notes. Perhaps she had a Dictaphone on the table that I couldn't see. Was she really interviewing him, I wondered? Well, if not, then what? What the hell was I getting at? I shook my head sharply – shuddered is probably a better description. Her story about Hector had really got to me, I could tell. The thought of them lying together in her bed in that studio flat on the Lower East Side... But, for God's sake, she wouldn't be interested in some old guy like *this* guy would she? Hector – she said Hector was older. Not this old... I tried to snap myself out of it. Of course she was interviewing him. This was her job. This was what she was here for. Of course she had a Dictaphone. What did I think she was doing? Somewhere a crow began cawing. I rubbed my eyes with the heels of my hands and tried to stop thinking about her and Hector. Her wedding day. What she'd said about Portugal – marrying into a Portuguese family... how could I compete with that? How could I even try? The way he somehow made her feel at home. And I am not stupid; I also wondered why she had chosen to tell me all this.

*

We had not really made good time on the way there that morning and the interview had taken longer than planned, so in the end it was after 9 p.m. when we finally got to our hotel. At the check-in desk the clerk seemed to take a while to find our reservation. "Oh, yes, here it is," he announced in the end: "one double room."

"Oh," said Lydia. "Is that..? I think we wanted two single beds. Is it two single beds?"

The clerk peered superfluously at his computer screen. "No," he said. "No, ma'am... A double bed."

"Did you..?" she asked me.

"Yes," I said to the clerk. "I definitely booked two single beds."

"Well, I'm very sorry about that, sir," he said, "but right now this is the only room we have."

"Do you have a rollaway?" asked Lydia.

He checked the computer. "I'm afraid someone's using it," he said, which under the circumstances somehow seemed a graphic way of putting it.

We made our way up the stairs in silence. Our room was in the attic under a pitched roof so low that I couldn't stand upright, and twice I banged my head, once painfully. Lydia got changed in the bathroom while I waited in bed a little nervously, and when she came out, wearing a pair of very chaste and unrevealing pyjamas and some unseasonably thick socks, she avoided my eyes as she got in beside me and turned out the light.

In the morning I woke up to find that, to my surprise, she was lying asleep against my chest. I pulled her a little closer and stroked her shoulder gently, wondering if she had put her arms around me consciously or in her sleep. Her body was soft against mine, her skin warm under my fingertips. I closed my eyes and settled back into a happy doze. From the window, through the stuttering sounds of the small town's Sunday rituals, came a scuffling noise, and I half-opened my eyes to see a small bird sitting in the gap between the ledge and the sash window, facing quizzically out towards the road. As I watched, it turned to me, and suddenly with a sickening lurch I realised that it had a tiny human head, dominated by a pair of huge, hypnotic black eyes. I struggled up in shock, and Lydia awoke, saying, "What? What's wrong?" but my sudden movements had frightened it and it had already flapped away. I sat back, leaning on my elbows. "What's wrong?" Lydia said again. "What is it?" Sweat began to trickle down from my hairline. But how could I say what it was, even to her? It was a ba.

*

We didn't talk much on the way back to Manhattan. She watched the road again, and I tried not to think about what I'd seen at the window. When we got home and tried to park in the car park beneath the building, the Peacocks' space had been taken by an enormous Ford station wagon, and we circled around for a while before parking in the closest spot we could find. Lydia was nervous.

"They'll never know," I reassured her. "Come on – who remembers where they park?"

We rose in the elevator in silence, and parted with a hug and a couple of European kisses at our separate front doors, bags in hand. I wanted to invite her in. I wanted to lie in bed with her again with my arms around her as we had that morning in Horseheads. I wasn't usually so hesitant about things like this, but with Lydia somehow I felt I just didn't know quite how to move things on to that next step. I turned away in frustration. She disappeared behind her door.

Inside the Peacocks' apartment, the heating had come on for some reason, and the place was blazing. I took my shirt off and lay on my bed in the dark looking out across the flat roof at New York and thinking about the wonderful feeling of her body against my chest. A long strand of her dark brown hair had caught itself in the stubble of my jaw line and I gently detached it and turned it over loosely in my fingertips. Something was about to change between us – if I could just take the initiative, if I could just work out how...

It was a foggy night and out past the flat roof almost all the skyscrapers had disappeared into mist, just the odd coloured light blinking groggily here and there, and I suddenly felt exultantly what the New Yorkers of a hundred years ago must have felt, two hundred, three hundred, that this island and this city was theirs to create from scratch. I watched the trees of Central Park rustle and sway as a warm wind blew in from the Hudson. It was something that had been happening for hundreds of years, thousands, ever since Manhattan Island first rose up from the ice – and I knew then, knew with total certainty, that somehow I would find a way to reach her, and I couldn't sleep afterwards for hours thinking about it, my mind racing unstoppably on in a mad whirl of excitement and anticipation.

Chapter 6

That week Samuel Latza finally got around to giving out that promotion, and to noticeable disgruntlement from some of my colleagues he pronounced that it would go to me. My responsibilities immediately started to expand, and by that Friday, I was already helping organise a book launch for one of our artists at MoMA. Afterwards, Lydia arrived to meet me; I introduced her to Latza and once he'd left we toasted my new job with free champagne and took a night-time tour of the galleries together. That night she was dressed almost like a biker, in a leather jacket, tight jeans and high heels, a completely new image. As always she was the most beautiful woman in the room – I knew it without even looking around. We wandered the galleries, and I watched her reflected in the endlessly repeating mirrors of Yayoi Kusama's Infinity Mirrored Room, a hundred of her, a thousand, a million. We stopped for a while at Lawrence Weiner's 'A Wall Pitted by a Single Air Rifle Shot' and talked about the damage the young Jeffrey had caused with his airgun to his aunts' hallway wall. On the floor above there was another Peacock connection: a version of Edward Hazlemere's 'The Weighing of the Heart.' We gazed at the distended eyes of the Devourer and the aluminium tinting on the heart as it sat in the scale.

"This must be the original," I said. "Are you sure the one the Peacocks have is not a print?"

"Look at the label," she said, pointing. "He created a number of different versions. This is one of them, and I think I've seen one in LA at the Lacma... and somehow the Peacocks have one. I asked them about it when I first saw it, and Marie said, 'Oh, we bought that a long time ago, dear... when we were rich...'"

I laughed. In the gift shop they were selling life-size prints of the Hazlemere painting, with glistening silver paint on the heart to match the original.

"We should get one," I said. "You could put it up in your apartment. Or I'll put it up in my room. We could frame it just like theirs. It would blow their minds."

She seemed to find this quite funny, so to prolong the joke I bought one of the prints. "Or we could steal theirs and replace it with this one," I continued as the shop assistant wrapped it up.

She laughed again. "They'd never know it was gone," she said.

I was really enjoying myself, but unfortunately on the way out we happened to pass a small display dedicated to Martin Samarkos, along with a black and white (pretentiously retro) picture of the artist himself grinning like an idiot with Glenn Lowry, and that put me in a bad mood. He seemed to be going from strength to strength, I admitted through gritted teeth. I recalled the last time I had seen him, at a slightly drunken Bougainville party two or three years earlier, when I ended up telling him rudely: "You've only got one style. You only do one thing. I'm totally bored of it."

"But people aren't bored of buying it, my embittered friend!" he had replied gleefully.

In June, as the temperature steadfastly refused to improve, the Peacock sisters packed up for a two-week jaunt to the Caribbean. "It's this darn weather, young Nicholas," Marie explained, shaking her head conspiratorially as the rain beat hard against the windowpanes. "Rose can't *stand* it..."

Rose told me much the same about Marie. I helped them downstairs with their luggage and wove between the lanes of Fifth Avenue traffic to flag them down a cab. "Forty-five dollars plus tip..." murmured Rose wonderingly as they got in, seemingly seeing the flat fare to the airport printed on the back of the driver's seat through new eyes. "This must seem a tremendously expensive city to you, young man."

"Actually I think the taxis are quite cheap here," I said. "Back in London black cab drivers charge the earth."

Rose looked momentarily horrified. "Young Nicholas," she said nervously, her brow knotted. "I really do have to tell you that in this country we try to avoid making those kinds of sweeping statements based on race, no matter how justified you, or I, might feel they are..."

"No, I meant–" I began.

"It's all right, dear," she said, shutting the door of the cab and rolling down the window. "You're among friends here. But for God's sake be careful who you *say* these things to, Nicholas. Colleagues of mine have been locked up for less."

Hyo-Sonn was cancelled for the duration, so I had the place completely to myself, and the air seemed to settle slowly like a sigh of relief after the door shut behind them. One evening, at a loose end, I decided to try to have another look at 'The Weighing of the Heart', so I went to the bear's paw box and dug out the large key, but I was surprised and disappointed to find that when I tried to open the study door with it, it didn't work. I stood in front of the locked door for a while, thinking about the painting inside and my conversation with Lydia in the MoMA gift shop.

The weather had cleared completely almost as soon as the Peacocks had left, and one night, finishing work rather late, I decided it would be almost criminal to reject the deep reddish-brown colours of the streets at sunset for the juddering shadows of the subway, so I began walking north up Broadway and thought I'd see how far I got before I got too tired. I moseyed happily along until at the junction with Lispenard Street something slightly unpleasant tugged at my memory, and I stopped. The bar across the street – wasn't that the place where Lydia had said she used to work? A fat, bearded man in a baseball cap shuffled furtively towards its blacked-out front door from a dirty-looking basement video shop across the street, and I recalled Marty Gamble staring hungrily at Lydia's short skirt in the lobby of our building as he'd looked her up and down. I crossed the street. I wanted to see what they had the barmaids wear in there. I pushed open the door.

The bar was dank and grimy, long and thin, and dense with an impenetrable atmosphere I felt instantly I was not invited to be part of. Thick pipes ran along the ceilings, and there was graffiti on the wood-panelled walls. In the far corner a man in a blue suit was bellowing stock prices into his cellphone, and I ignored him and concentrated instead on the barmaids. What did they wear? White tank-tops that crossed their otherwise bare backs in an X, short black skirts, and red stockings with bows above the knee. I watched them walk from the bar to the tables, or stretch to reach the overhead racks of beer glasses. One of them was Hispanic and if I squinted my eyes a little – She turned around, and, wait, Jesus, hold on – it was her, it was Lydia... I stood half way up in my seat, spilling my beer, mortified that she'd caught me in there. She began to move towards me and I rose to meet her, my mind rushing to compose a story about passing by and feeling thirsty suddenly, not knowing that this was the bar where she worked, and as she got closer another waitress crossed in front of her, carrying a tray to a table, and when the second waitress moved away I saw that there was nobody there. I put my drink down and left immediately, and struggled home under the slowly-cooling embers of the sun.

Edward Hazlemere died and there were long articles about him in the New York Times and the Wall Street Journal, and Lydia and I read them together in the Peacocks' kitchen over coffee, his painting just two rooms away from us in the locked study. He had been a curator at the Metropolitan Museum's Arts of Ancient Egypt galleries, and, unknown to his colleagues, to his family, his friends, throughout the 50s had been creating his own versions of dozens of the museum's most striking Egyptian artworks, working with photography, paint and screen-print in a room in the basement of the Met in the evenings after he had finished work. His pictures had been created in total secrecy until 1957 or '58, when a senior colleague chanced upon him working on one of them one night. After some toing and froing, Hazlemere was persuaded to allow ten of the paintings to be put on display in a small vacant gallery at the Met. Unexpectedly, the exhibition was a huge hit and after two weeks it was moved to a bigger space. At his next exhibition, later that year, Hazlemere showed twenty pictures, including his now well-known portraits of Akhenaten and Anubis, his works depicting Bes, the protector of households, and that vast, almost never-ending field of blue-glazed shabtis that established his radical approach to perspective. The show also included what was to become his most celebrated painting, 'Coming Forth by Day', an enormous depiction of a ba with its wings spread wide as it soared out of its tomb, as well as a version of 'The

Weighing of the Heart' that was immediately bought by MoMA – the one Lydia and I had seen there a few weeks earlier. Hazlemere never left his job at the Met, and only dropped down to part-time with extreme reluctance once his paintings started changing hands for colossal sums in the 1980s. Along with its article about his death, the Journal published a list of his most valuable works; 'Coming Forth by Day' was of course the most expensive, but one of the versions of 'The Weighing of the Heart' had apparently sold the previous year in Dubai for nearly five hundred thousand dollars.

"Lucky Peacocks," said Lydia pensively.

"I tried to get into the study to see it the other day," I said, and told her about attempting to use the key from the bear's paw box.

"No luck?" she asked, looking down at a photograph of the painting in the Wall Street Journal. "Reading all this – I'd love to see it again. Maybe you got the wrong key."

"Yes, maybe," I said, and then thought of another option. "Maybe we can see it through the window from Rose's library."

We went upstairs to the library, brushing dead bees off the windowsill, and tried to look down from the balcony into the study window beneath, but in vain.

"Oh, well," said Lydia, sitting down next to me on the sofa as she had done when we had leafed through Rose's books a few weeks earlier. "What are all these bees?" she asked.

"I don't know," I said. "They're everywhere."

There was a story about Ra weeping and his tears falling to earth as bees, and I began to talk about that, but she seemed to have something on her mind and so after a while we lapsed into silence. I had just decided I should try to make a move and bring things to a head once and for all, for good or ill, and I was reaching out to touch her arm, not quite sure what I would do after that, when she said: "I've been talking to Samuel Latza about making a print of my painting of Queen Nefertiti."

"Samuel Latza?" I asked, bewildered. "What do you mean?"

"He saw me in the lobby the other day and we got talking," she said. "I told him about my work, and he seemed interested, so he came up to take a look and he really liked my Nefertiti painting."

"What? When was this?"

"The other day. Last week," she said.

"He came up?" I asked.

"He says if I have a screen-print made up, say a series of seventy-five, he'll sell them in the gallery and put the original on display there too. He said he'd sell the original too if I wanted, but I'm not sure I want to."

"He came up? He was in your bedroom?"

"He was in – we mostly spoke in the kitchen," she said. "But he wanted to see the painting, so... He talked about you a lot. He seems to really rate you," she said.

I was quiet. "Well, are you – are you going to do it?" I asked.

"It costs a lot of money," she said. "To get the screen-prints printed. I mean, it would cost about six thousand dollars for the whole run. It's a lot of colours. I just haven't got that kind of money. But I'm thinking about it."

We were quiet for a while after that and soon afterwards she went home. I lay on my bed in a silent agony of frustration. I didn't know how much longer I could stand this. I needed to do something; needed to do something before somebody like Latza, some older guy, probably, somebody like Latza or that film director in Horseheads or Marty Gamble or whoever, took her away from me for good. I turned over on my side and looked out across the roof garden towards her kitchen, where a lamp burnt painfully in the darkness.

*

And then one day I managed to get the study door open. I had decided to give the large key from the bear's paw box one more go, and as I turned and twisted it in the mechanism from right to left, clicking and clacking it one way or the other, I suddenly felt that something was about to give, and, encouraged, I hoisted the body of the door slightly up on its hinges, particles of dust and rust cascading along the seam of the frame, and redoubled my efforts. The key fought against the lock and pressed itself painfully into the flesh of my fingers, and just as I felt either it or they were in danger of snapping in two, the lock twisted heavily into place and the door fell open. I paused there, watching the crack of light where the door lay slightly ajar shimmer and glow in the breeze from an open window somewhere, and then I pushed it open all the way, and walked quietly to the centre of the room and looked up at 'The Weighing of the Heart.'

I had read quite a bit about it since I had seen it last. Seven versions exist, or did then: a relief and six works on canvas, of which this was one, and Hazlemere also made an etching of the same scene, now fairly valuable in its own right, although reaching nothing like the prices of the paintings. It was sunny and warm in the study and I sat at the Peacocks' desk for a while, looking at the painting, which was truly a beautiful thing: the way Anubis's hand seemed to be just about to let go of the weighing scales, the way the Devourer was visibly struggling to control itself, struggling to stop itself leaping forward to begin its horrendous feast.

As soon as I saw Lydia's kitchen light on a couple of hours later I crossed the roof garden and knocked on her door. "I've got something to show you," I said, and took her by the hand into the Peacocks' apartment and into the study.

She walked straight to the canvas, peering closely at a screen-print element in the background, and then at the aluminium paint on the heart. "It's a wonderful painting," she said, standing back and taking it in as a whole.

"Yes," I said.

"Are you hungry?" she asked after a minute or so, turning around.

I looked across at her and back to the painting. "We could swap them now," I said.

She laughed. "Swap them? What do you mean?"

"The print I bought from MoMA. It's in my room," I said, pointing out towards the hallway. I brought it in, unwrapped it and held it up against the frame. It was almost exactly the same size, and the metallic paint on the heart duplicated the aluminium on the original almost perfectly.

"Let's get some dinner," she said.

At dinner I ordered too much wine. I felt excited. I had left a copy of the Complete Shakespeare and a Merriam-Webster dictionary propping open the study door, in case it somehow locked itself again. The Peacocks would be back from the Caribbean in a couple of days. This was really our only chance. I told Lydia we'd be in the Caribbean ourselves soon, once we'd sold this painting, probably on our own yacht. I told her she'd have enough money to get her screen-print made up. I told her I had a contact who could help us sell it, a guy I went to art school with who might be able to–

"I know a couple of people in El Barrio," she said quietly, to my surprise.

"What do you mean?" I asked.

"I was asking around because I have that Jörg Sasse print. I was thinking about selling it to help pay for my screen-print. So I asked around. Some people I know..." she said. I poured us both some more wine. "Are we really going to do this?" she asked almost silently.

I looked at her and held her gaze, and then slowly reached out my hand across the table, all the time still looking her in the eye. She looked down at my hand, and there was a pause that seemed to go on for a very long time while she decided whether to take it. And then she took my hand.

"Yes," she said, looking at me. "Yes."

*

We went back to the apartment slightly intoxicated, Lydia leaning against me in the elevator. Without talking about it she followed me into the Peacocks' study, and I took the painting off the wall, laid it on the desk and began to remove the back, pulling the nails out with a pair of pliers from the laundry room. Using just my fingertips, I carefully slid the canvas out and passed it to Lydia. On the reverse was a half-completed sketch of the outlines of Anubis, Thoth and, faintest of all, the Devourer; probably no one had seen it for decades. I picked up the MoMA print from the floor beside me and fitted it into the frame, slotting the backing board back into place and hammering the nails in again as close to their old positions as I could manage. Then I hung it up on the wall, and we both stood back and looked at it. It looked just the same. It looked exactly the same.

"Maybe we'd better – maybe we'd better put this in your apartment for now," I whispered, gingerly picking up the original painting, and she nodded, and we made our way over the flat roof to her apartment, and we slid the painting carefully under her bed, and then I kissed her, lips on dry lips, both kneeling beside the bed with our fingers still on the edge of the painting, and I pulled her on to the bed, and she began to kiss me desperately then, like someone coming up for air, and I pushed her dress up around her waist and we had sex as the painting burned and glowed beneath us. The Egyptians believed that the heart, not the brain, was the source of intellect, mind, and conscience – mine showed no pangs of guilt whatsoever. I held her in my arms, and she held me in her arms, and I thought of how the ba and the body would hold each other when they reunited after death, the body's arms tight around the ba, the ba's wings wrapped around the body's chest. And the painting seemed to cry out beneath the bed, silver rivulets running like tears.

Chapter 7

I woke up confused, her naked body wrapped around me, her face pressed against my chest. Upstairs I could hear movement: chairs scraping back and forth, heavy objects being placed on bedside tables and in closets. Their voices seemed slower than usual, tired, perplexed, but there was no doubting who it was: the Peacocks were back. Had we locked the study door? We had, I was sure of it. But I lay there nevertheless in a fog of nervousness as they paced from room to room above us, Lydia asleep beside me. Gradually she opened her eyes, and when I stroked her hair, still listening to the Peacocks, she pressed herself tightly against me, and kissed my neck. And then suddenly she froze, and I knew that she had heard the Peacocks too.

I saw them briefly that evening, when I came home from work. They were exhausted and depressed after their holiday, and preparing to move on to Long Island ahead of schedule that night. Frannie was asleep upside down on the sofa with her eyes open, a slightly disturbing sight. By the morning they were gone.

I met up with Lydia that night on the flat roof. She was sober now. "We had better put that painting back," she said. "Have you still got the key?"

I took her into the living room and we retrieved it from the bear's paw box. She tried the handle of the study door, and then I put the key in the lock and tried to reproduce the sequence of twists and turns I had used to unlock it the day before. I used my shoulder as leverage and tried to lift the door up on its hinges – but nothing.

"Let me try," she said, and she rattled the key fruitlessly east and west for a while. "How did you do it?" she asked, frustrated.

"I – it sort of – it lifted slightly," I said. I took her place and tried again. But nothing. She looked at me. I put the key back in the box and we went back out on to the roof in silence. She got out a packet of cigarettes and silently offered me one, and we smoked together like that for a while in the evening sunlight.

"The print..." she said in the end. "You really couldn't tell, could you? You really couldn't tell it wasn't the real thing?"

"It looked just the same," I said, although I wished I could check. We were quiet again.

"I really do know someone who could help us sell it," she said.

"Do you?" I said.

"I don't know how much we'll get for it," she said. "Much less than it's worth."

"But still..." I said.

"Nick..." she said then. "The Peacocks... They've been so good to me..."

"They'll never know," I said. "They'll never find out."

"Yes," she said doubtfully. I reached for her hand and held it for a while, and then I leaned over and we began to kiss. It felt like I had been waiting my whole life to do this. She held on to me very tightly and I slid my hand up the back of her top.

Suddenly the light came on in the laundry room and we broke apart, startled – terrified, even. "Hello?" I shouted. The back door opened. Hyo-Sonn stood in the doorway.

"Mr Nick," she said. "Miss Peacock asked me to move in for a while."

"Move in?" I asked in utter incomprehension.

"Move in," she said. "Miss Peacock says she wants more cleaning, more ironing, more meals. She asked me to move in to the house. I will sleep in the library. She gave me blankets for the couch," she added.

"For how long?" I asked.

She shrugged. "Stay until Miss Peacock says go," she said. "Would you like a drink? Miss Lydia? Coffee?"

"No, no thanks," I said.

"No, no thank you, Hyo-Sonn," said Lydia. Hyo-Sonn disappeared back inside, leaving the back door open, and we could hear her bustling about in the kitchen, making coffee for herself.

"That's strange," I said.

*

Weeks went by, and we forgot about the painting, almost, as it lay below us, under the bed, dormant, while we spent our evenings, nights, weekends above it wrapped up blissfully in the start of our new life together. I was spending more and more time at Lydia's, feeling much less comfortable at the Peacocks' now Hyo-Sonn was living there too. I lay in Lydia's bed happily each morning after she had gone to work, utterly content, basking in the summer sun that burst stunningly through the window at around 7 a.m., projecting the blazing image of the windowpanes on to her bedroom wall. The Egyptians believed that the sun died each night and was born anew every morning – and that was exactly how I felt. I would have a shower in her tiny bathroom, trying not to bump my head on the low ceiling, then wander back across the roof to the Peacocks', where Hyo-Sonn would make me a cup of coffee as I got ready for work.

"I saw that guy from El Barrio yesterday," Lydia said one morning as she was getting dressed.

"What guy?" I asked.

She stopped, and looked at me. "The one who can... who can help us with the painting," she said. It was the first time we had mentioned it for quite a while.

"Oh," I said. "So... so what does he think?"

"He was in a café near my studio," she said. "He was helping some movers down there. He stopped and had a coffee with me."

"And what did he say?" I asked.

"He's not sure," she said. "He knows a guy who knows a guy... But he thought he could probably help."

"Okay," I said, sitting up in bed a bit. "Okay. So now what?"

"This guy," she said, not looking at me. "He's not really a friend of mine. He's a friend – He's more a friend of Hector's. And the people he knows, he says they have to hear it from Hector before they'll agree."

"From Hector?" I said. It was the first time I'd

said his name. "But Hector's got nothing to do with this."

She sat on the edge of the bed and took my hand. "I think we shouldn't keep that painting where it is for much longer."

"No," I said. "I agree."

"We could always try again to put it back," she said, watching for my reaction. "We could try the key again."

I thought about this, thought about the fact that she was sitting here half-dressed in front of me holding my hand, thought about waking up holding her that morning and going to bed with her that night. "I don't want to put it back," I said truthfully. "Do you?" I asked her. "What do you think?"

She was quiet for a while. "I'm worried about it under the bed," she said in the end. "I'm worried Hyo-Sonn could find it, the Peacocks could find it, anything could happen. And I seem to be telling myself it would be too difficult to put it back – that we wouldn't be able to get the key to work, that the door's only unlocked when the two of them are at home. But really, I'm sure we would find a way. And the more I think about it, the more I realise – I don't want us to put it back. The more I think about it, the more I realise that what I really think is that we've done it now... we've done it now and – and I can't stop thinking about the money, really, what it said it was worth, in the newspaper – what we could do with even some of that kind of money. My artwork – what it would mean for my artwork. It would really change things for me. I could cut down on my journalism, I could finish some prints and start selling them and put a show on somewhere. This could really get things started for me."

I nodded.

After a pause, she added, "I've asked Hector if we can meet up to talk about it."

"Meet up?" I said. "Wait a minute. I don't want Hector to know about this. I don't want him to be involved in this."

"It's okay," she said. "We can trust him. I trust him."

I was quiet for a while – brooding is probably the word. "So where do we meet him?" I said in the end. She looked alarmed and abruptly dropped my hand. "No no no, you can't come, you can't be there," she said. "He can't know about you; he'll go crazy. Oh God, I'll meet him on my own, Nick; are you crazy?"

She left for work and I lay in bed, watching a thin line of reflected blue light race along the top of the windowpane as a police car went by far below. A headache passed gradually over my skull like a cloud across the moon, and I looked up at the picture of

Queen Nefertiti that she had painted for him for their wedding day. It sneered at me languidly. It was like he was looking right at me.

*

The evening Hector came round to Lydia's apartment I waited in the Peacocks' darkened kitchen and watched the reflection of her windows in the huge panes of glass across the street. She was waiting for him in the kitchen, sipping at a coffee. The intercom buzzer rang, and half a minute later I heard the elevator arrive in the corridor and she got up and walked along the hallway to the front door and let him in. Then they reappeared in the reflection of her kitchen window. He sat at the table, looking supremely comfortable and at home, and she busied herself getting him a drink, looking back over her shoulder from the work surface as they chatted.

It was frustrating to see them in reflection, and difficult to tell what was going on; I wanted to get a better look, so I quietly slid the laundry room door open and made my way out on to the flat roof, gingerly moving closer and closer to the small square window set in the top of her kitchen door. I could see Hector sitting at the table, leaning back in his chair, drinking a beer from a thin glass, nodding his minuscule head seriously as Lydia spoke. He was wearing jeans and a red and black zip-up jacket. She was wearing a thin, pale sweater that was slightly see-through and a belt of beads that jangled quietly as she moved. She was leaning against the sink, holding her coffee cup in both hands, but as she spoke to him she suddenly moved forward and sat down in the seat opposite him, leaning towards him now, and I noticed he still wore his wedding ring, despite their divorce. My face was close to the glass. They were speaking in Portuguese and of course I couldn't understand what they were saying, but it was easy enough to follow the flow of the conversation. Lydia was speaking quickly, seeming slightly upset or agitated; Hector's voice was low, soothing, and he looked her in the eye at all times. It gradually calmed her down. Then he spoke for quite a long time. She began to smile, at first sadly, and then more unequivocally. He reached out his hand, and she moved away, but still smiling. They both got up after that and went into the bedroom, causing my heart to lurch in sudden pain like a knee twisting in its socket. But they came out half a minute later holding the Hazlemere painting and laid it out carefully on the kitchen table, the aluminium paint on the heart glistening under the kitchen lights. Hector was asking her a series of questions and thoughtfully digesting the answers. She smiled; she looked grateful. He raised both hands in a gesture I couldn't quite understand and assumed a grave expression. And then she reached towards him and they hugged, and I found myself taking an involuntary step backwards, feeling suddenly that I was intruding on something I could never be a part of, and I moved back into the shadows of the Peacocks' apartment and waited for her to call me.

*

She said Hector had told her we could get something like three hundred thousand dollars for the painting, with his friends taking ten percent. But she had to go with his friends that Saturday to arrange the sale, and she didn't know when she would be back. It might even be the next day. And she wasn't sure exactly where they were going. I said to her, "Text me where you are. Every time they drive you somewhere new, text me where you are."

"I will," she said.

They came and picked her up just after lunch in a red minivan. It slowed to a halt on Fifth Avenue, she got in the back, and it sped away. I watched it until I could no longer see it. It was pouring with rain out like a monsoon, had been ever since the Peacocks got back from the Caribbean, more or less. The heady smell of a coffee-roasting factory wafted in from across the river in Queens.

She didn't come back for two days. I waited in a state of some anxiety. I didn't receive any texts from her. I didn't receive any phone calls. I paced the apartment, going out on to the roof to watch a wild, billowing summer storm rattle and shake the trees of Central Park like a chain-link fence, my clothes wet through and sticking to my skin. There was an awful cracking sound as two black branches flung themselves loose, bounced against their fellows, and fell heavily to the ground. I hoped no one was hurt.

I paced from room to room, turned the bathroom light off, opened the window in the kitchen, stared across at her empty apartment.

I accepted coffees and meals from Hyo-Sonn, put my clothes on hangers, used a spirit level I found in the laundry room to check all my pictures had been hung up straight, took a frame apart and cut my finger on the jagged edge of the glass, patched up a hole in the arm of one of my shirts with the Peacocks' sewing kit, turned the bathroom light off, and went to bed.

I slept alone in my own room for the first time in weeks, the moon bouncing like a ball at the window.

Something crept on to my neck and I slapped it away. A door slammed out in the corridor and I heard Marty Gamble talking on his cellphone, his voice gradually fading away as he headed to the elevator. To distract myself I went up to the Bronx Zoo, but when one of the Nile crocodiles rose from its swamp-like pit, I saw that the grey-green of its rugged, indestructible, primordial scales gave way below the waterline to the smooth golden-yellow of a lion's mane and the pinkish hue of a pair of enormous trunk-like back legs.

The second night, when Lydia had still not returned, I phoned her, texted her and emailed her, but there was no reply, and I went to bed murmuring one of those Egyptian spells from 'The Book of the Dead' that could be used to protect the living: "If this text is used on earth, he will not be exposed by the messengers who attack those who commit wrong in all the earth. His head shall not be cut off, he shall not be destroyed by the knife of Seth. He shall not be carried off to any prison. But he shall enter the tribunal and come forth justified. He shall be preserved from the fear of wrongdoing that exists in all the earth." But the whole thing was really supposed to be said over an image of a snake drawn in dried myrrh, so who knows if it really worked?

Outside on the Monday morning when I left the

building to go to work I felt something bang against my back, and I turned around to see two tiny figures disappear behind a car. I bent down and glanced under the vehicle and saw four little feet swaddled in enormous sneakers bubbling with gimmicks and logos, and walked out into the road to discover two mop-topped young boys with their backs pressed against the car doors.

"Can I help you?" I asked.

"Sorry, mister," said one, pointing over my shoulder. "My dad just..." And they spotted a slight break in the traffic and dashed across Fifth Avenue and into the park.

I tried to phone her again that lunchtime, walking around the block by the courthouse; it went straight to voicemail. I stopped outside a café to leave a message, ducking under the awning out of the breeze. As I spoke I gazed unseeingly into the café window, and there, sitting by himself, was a man in his sixties with long grey hair and row upon row of tiny black teeth. It was the director Lydia had interviewed in Horseheads, I was sure of it. And at the counter, looking up at the menu board, was a young Latina woman in an eggshell-blue dress. I hung up my call and burst in through the café door, but when she turned around it wasn't Lydia at all, but actually a lady I sometimes saw going in and out of the court building as I passed by each day, and, when I turned to look for the director, there was nobody there.

*

She was sitting on the flat roof when I got back from work that night, looking out towards the park, doing nothing, not even smoking. I opened the laundry room door and she turned towards me and gave me a wan smile. I touched her on the shoulder as I sat down beside her, and she kissed me politely on the cheek.

"How are you?" I asked, my mouth dry. It felt like we hadn't seen each other for months.

"Okay," she said.

"You – You sold it?"

"Yes," she said, still looking out towards the park, where the trees whistled and whipped in the wind.

"Where have you been?" I asked.

"Look," she said. "I think – I'm not trying to keep secrets from you. But they... they said don't tell anyone where they – So I think it's probably best if I..."

"I was worried about you out God-knows-where all alone," I said.

"I wasn't on my own," she said.

"What do you – what do you mean?"

She was silent.

"Who was with you?" I asked.

"Hector," she said in the end.

"What?"

"He came with me," she said. "He was worried about me, all right? These people were not – he *knew* them, but they're not exactly his best friends or anything and he was worried. Look, I think we should just – I'm back now. Can we just forget it ever happened?"

And she pulled a shoebox full of bank notes out of the carrier bag by her feet.

*

We lay on her bed leafing through the money. It was one hundred thousand dollars. Much less than the painting was worth, but she said they wouldn't pay more because of the danger in buying and selling such obviously stolen property, and at the time that seemed to make sense.

I counted the money out slowly on the duvet while Lydia dozed beside me. I didn't feel like I'd expected to feel. They went together to sell it. He was worried about her and he protected her, she said. Was that really why he went along? What was in it for him? Was she grateful? I couldn't bear to think about it. Where were they for two nights? I couldn't stop picturing her climbing up into the back of that red minivan. How many of them were in there? Did they rape her? Did they try to rape her? Did Hector stop them?

"He was worried about me, all right?"

He'd been protecting her from something, that much was clear. Well, good. Good that he protected her. Of course that was good. But why were they away for so long? Where had they stayed? If he was protecting her, presumably he must have stayed with her, at night, stayed in the same room as her. I pictured a scuzzy motel clipped on to the side of a colourless highway somewhere out in the vacant wastes of Pennsylvania or New Jersey, a yellowing mattress, a broken lamp, moth-ravaged curtains, lorries shaking the window frames as they pounded past. In the same bed? I wanted to ask her. In the same bed? But she had made it very clear on the roof that she didn't want to talk about it.

He obviously wanted her back. He obviously wanted me gone. She seemed to think he didn't know about me, but he knew all right. He must know. I had felt uncomfortable enough about her asking his advice, but now he was actually *involved*, now he had a hold over both of us. He was obviously still in love with her. And suddenly I realised that now he would have a simple way of getting rid of me and making sure his way was clear: he knew everything about the theft. Everything. He could give the police details on every aspect: how we stole it, who we sold it to, where it was now. Or forget the police – he only had to say one word to his friends, those compadres of his in El Barrio; only had to claim that the picture was a fake, that I'd tricked Lydia, that I'd ripped him and Lydia off; only had to tell them that and then one night, walking in front of the building, that red minivan would pull up, they'd bundle me in, and that would be it for me. Lydia began to stir, and in her half-sleep pressed herself up against me. Banknotes fluttered briefly into the air and then came to rest again.

"I wonder if we did the right thing," I said.

"We definitely didn't do the right thing," she said, her eyes still closed.

"We're rich," I said.

"Yes," she replied, adding: "The American Dream."

And we lay there sadly for a while.

Chapter 8

I began to arrive at the gallery later and later each day. There just didn't seem to be any point hurrying. I would lie in Lydia's bed after she had gone to work watching people walking their dogs in slow circuits on the roof across the street, remembering the feeling of her feet pressed between my two feet, of my hands at her waist, the small of her back, how she looked when she took her top off, her arms high up above her head, how she felt when she was asleep, our bodies pressed up close against each other, a tangle of tightly-held arms and legs. At night sometimes as she slept she would leap and twitch like a frightened animal, and I would stroke her shoulders and kiss the nape of her neck until she relaxed again.

I watched Marie Peacock going through her rent books and mortgage statements in the study through my half-open bedroom door as I towelled my hair dry after a shower, the shadow of her profile projected with alarming magnification on to the wall beside her by the angle-poise lamp on her desk. The print of 'The Weighing of the Heart' gleamed convincingly above her. If they were to discover what we'd done, the Peacocks would have to dismantle the frame and check what was in there – and why on earth would they ever do that? Perhaps if the frame broke, I thought suddenly, waves of burning-hot terror washing over me. But it was fixed to the wall in the traditional sturdy fashion: a line of thick twine attached to hooks on the back of the frame, hanging off a hefty, utilitarian steel screw. It had probably hung there indestructibly for fifty years. Why would it choose to fall off now? Frannie silently wound herself around my feet and turned her face up towards me, fangs bared.

I was starting to find it all quite stressful, and I began to be troubled by a recurring dream in which Lydia and I were looking for a lost ring on the boat from Boston to Provincetown. We couldn't find it anywhere, and the dream always ended with Lydia heading off to search for it in another part of the boat and then disappearing completely, at which point I would wake up, usually quite upset. The dream had some basis in reality; I had actually once travelled on the ferry from Boston to Provincetown, but not with Lydia, with Hannah. We had flown up to Boston for a few days' holiday soon after getting together, a successful trip that had helped us cement our developing relationship.

Hannah had told me beforehand that I would probably find Boston quite a European-looking city, with antiquated buildings and illogical higgledy-piggledy streets and so on, and it was true that there was a handsome old brickwork bridge over the Charles River that wouldn't have looked out of place in London or Berlin, and that the seventeenth-century graveyard where Paul Revere is buried is enjoyably untidy and disordered. But in my opinion the city still had the unmistakeably tough and unsentimental tang of America, that feeling that if an eighteen-wheel truck making an important delivery needed to get to a depot one day the residents would quite happily demolish the Cathedral of the Holy Cross to let it through, and concrete over Benjamin Franklin's birthplace to give it a bit of space to turn round.

Hannah had laughed at that. She'd found my sense of humour a real novelty when we first met, which had been very flattering. She asked where else I had visited in America so far.

"Nowhere, really," I said. "It's New York I like."

"I'll have to take you down to Johnstown one day," she said. "My hometown. Johnstown, Pennsylvania: that is one nook of America you will *not* want to miss out on. In Johnstown we have the world's steepest vehicular inclined plane. No kidding."

I laughed. "Are your parents still there?" I asked her.

"Oh yeah," she said. "They, like, practically run the place. My dad was like the mayor for fifteen years. His family were in the steel business and everything, way back. In the nineteenth century our company was the world's leading producer of barbed wire. That's another Johnstown fact. Hey. You asked."

"Are they... are they wealthy then?" I asked. (I had found Americans to be much less wary of questions like this than the British.)

She shrugged. "I don't know... I mean, look at this ring." She showed me the ring her parents had given her for her birthday. We were tucked into a corner of a café by the window and it caught the warm rays of the late spring sunshine as she turned it this way and that. "They're always giving me things like this." She looked doubtfully around at the other customers. "Maybe I shouldn't have brought it on this trip."

"You brought it to Arna Tambor's degree show in that parking lot under the Williamsburg Bridge the other night," I said.

"That's true," she said. We were always going to degree shows in parking lots under the Williamsburg

Bridge in those days.

We sat in silence for a little while, enjoying each other's company and our surroundings. It's always exciting at the beginning of a new relationship and I remember feeling happy to have invited her on this long weekend and looking forward to taking her back to our hotel that night. The coffee machine hissed and the hubbub of voices around us waxed and waned and waxed again. Across the road I could see floors of high-rise office life winding down for the day, four o'clock on a Friday, office staff marking time, the working week spinning slowly to a close. Girls sat perched on their friends' desks, reeling the evening in with a leisurely loop of conversation. I poured milk into my tea and it rushed up from the bottom and flooded to the surface, and we spent an agreeable few minutes sipping our drinks and watching a young driver trying to parallel park in an incredibly tight space right in front of the café. As so often in such cases, a number of men of various ages, races and social backgrounds immediately materialised from shops and residential buildings nearby in order to 'help' him.

"It's a tricky spot," I said generously to Hannah as he continued to struggle.

"He should have asked me," replied Hannah.

"Are you good?" I asked.

"Parallel parking? I'm the master," she said. "Once I pulled off this really tough spot in front of my dad – I felt like his son or something."

I laughed, and kissed her on the cheek.

We took the fast ferry out to Provincetown the next day, one and a half hours each way, out across the mouth of Cape Cod Bay, the arm of the peninsula sticking way out into the Atlantic, flexing its biceps, and as we walked along the dunes on the northern headland, buffeted by the ocean winds, I found myself, most unusually, thinking of England, staring out into the haze of blue sky and blue sea overlapping white at the horizon. Most of the time, in Manhattan, surrounded by New York on all sides, the subway below me, the skyscrapers above me, it was hard to believe England still existed. But here I felt I could almost see it, out east across the thousands of miles of ocean following the curve of the earth. Unsettled, I closed my eyes and turned away, and the feeling soon dissipated. We sat on a bench beside clapboard houses eating ice creams, looking at lighthouses and weighing up whether or not to climb the Pilgrim Monument, a gust of wind or a passer-by forcing flocks of gulls up into the sky at intervals with a brisk beat of wings.

That night on the way back to Boston we stood at the prow of the boat holding tight to the white front rail as the blisteringly powerful headwind tore through our hair and billowed up our clothes like sails. It felt reckless to be facing the elements head-on like that; it felt like the wind would only have to twist slightly one way or another and we would be flicked up and off the deck and would vanish for ever in the blur of the sea. A storm was gathering ahead of us, over Boston, and we watched as it circled and swooped over the silhouetted city until after an ominous pause it began to strike the buildings with sharp and terrifying bursts of lightning.

"Oh, God, did I drop it?" she said suddenly.

"What?" I asked. She was looking at her hands.

"My ring – did I drop it?" She stepped back from the rail and looked down at the deck. "The wind – did the wind catch it?" she said.

I began to look around. Hannah leant over the rail and stared apprehensively into the churning, roiling swell of the ocean. We looked all around the prow, and then retraced our steps around the boat, with increasing pessimism.

"I definitely had it when I got on the boat, because I took it off when I washed my hands in the bathroom," she said.

"Did you definitely put it back on?"

"I did, I remember I did," she said. "But I've checked in there anyway and it's not in there."

I asked the barman if he would let us know if anything was handed in, and left him my phone number, but I don't think either of us felt very hopeful. Just before the boat reached Boston, Hannah and I returned to the prow and she gazed sadly overboard.

"It must have come off when we were holding the rail," she said. "It must have come off my finger. It was never a very tight fit, on my finger. It must have dropped off into the sea. Oh dear. Mom will be disappointed."

"Oh dear," I said, pulling her into the circle of my arm. To cheer her up I took her out that night to a very well-reviewed seafood restaurant in the North End, and by the end of the evening she had almost forgotten about it. And I thought I had, too; after all, it was many years ago now. But perhaps sometimes these memories are buried closer to the surface than we think.

*

Slowly, we started to enjoy our money. Lydia took her painting of Queen Nefertiti to a printmaker recommended by Samuel Latza and they planned a screen-print run of one hundred. She bought me a stylish blue shirt and a linen blazer from a tiny shop she knew hidden away under a nondescript apartment block in Kips Bay. I wanted to take her to the restaurant at the top of the Chrysler Building, and we sat at our shining art-deco table amid the arching, echoing roof beams and Egyptian motifs and ate charcoal-grilled saddle of roe deer, black Perigord truffles and sake-steamed monkfish liver; after dessert, I took her hand and led her to one of the leaning triangular windowpanes, and we gazed down through the dusk at the streets and the grid, the rivers and the park, at the fire escapes clinging on to the blocks for dear life. Down below, in the tangle of Times Square, the cabs were roaring off their marks when the lights turned green and switching lanes with terrifying abandon. They swept along the overpass in front of Grand Central and swung recklessly around it like a diverted river.

"Look at the roof," said Lydia, smiling, pointing down at the softly glowing emerald green of the oxidised copper that covered the station, invisible at street level, invisible to those dashing hurriedly along the sidewalks under the streetlights. Towards home we could see the ragged buildings in front of the park, windows sparkling, plate glass reflecting the last fragments of the sunset, the sheets of offices hanging high above the rushing streets. I watched her track the progress of a car down Lexington Avenue, looking deep into the wells of the city streets. The enormous country was spread out behind us and New York was leading it like the prow of a ship.

"I'm really happy," I said.

"I'm glad," she said, still looking at the view, and I squeezed her hand tight.

*

We met up in the bar of the Waldorf-Astoria one night after we had both been working in our studios and chatted quietly in the lush calm and drank champagne and gradually ate our way through the tasting menu as a pianist played a white grand piano, and a singer in his sixties sang tremulously in a low tenor, starting with 'Breakfast in Bed' by Dusty Springfield and then moving on to 'Love Me' by Elvis Presley. A napkin rose from the table and blew away towards the patio doors at the far side of the room. Lydia seemed tired, and when we finished our meal I went over to reception to ask them to get us a cab and then realised there was a much easier solution and asked them to get us a room instead.

"Would you like to stay in the hotel, sir, or the towers?" the receptionist asked.

"Which is more expensive?" I asked.

"Oh, the towers," she said.

147

"The towers, please," I said.

*

Up in our suite we looked out from the balcony at the serrated skyline, the outlines of the buildings lit only by a creamy white moon, the city pausing with careful precision as if it were waiting for something, and then suddenly like a pistol going off or the blade of a guillotine slamming into place the sky was rent by a blaze of colour and noise, and Lydia gripped hold of my arm and of course, of course – it was the Fourth of July, and neither of us had given it a second thought. Lydia shook her head and smiled, and we sat on the balcony with another bottle of champagne as the fireworks exploded around us for hours, roman candles and Catherine wheels, waterfalls and skyrockets, helicopters and flares and fountains, and after that we watched them from bed for a while, and had sex as the balcony doors clinked together in the late-night breeze. But afterwards she seemed upset and turned away from me.

"What's wrong?" I asked her, stroking her hair.

"I don't know..." she said. "The Peacocks... We shouldn't have done it. We shouldn't have taken it. They've been so good to me."

"They'll never miss it," I said. "They'll never

know it's gone. They have so many paintings. And think about how that money's helping you. Your prints... They're going to be wonderful. This is really going to be great for you."

"I know," she said, crying slightly. "I know... but still."

I said I would go downstairs and get some more champagne. That would cheer her up.

"They'll send it up," she said, wiping her eyes.

"It's okay," I said. "I don't mind going." I put my clothes on and descended in the silent, gilt-edged elevator, and got out at reception, which was glowing gently like a log fire, and on impulse I turned and walked across the diamond-shaped floor tiles to the jewellery counter, where engagement rings glinted and glittered through the glass. None of them had price tags. I picked the one I thought looked the most exciting and paid for it in cash. The saleswoman didn't bat an eyelid.

I went back upstairs, where Lydia was now sitting on the balcony in her hotel robe, carefully laying out the four initial proofs of her Queen Nefertiti print on the table, each one using only a single colour: red, blue, yellow and black, producing strange, unexpected effects. Slightly clumsily – it's not quite as easy as it looks – I got down on one knee and took her hand and asked her to marry me. She looked away nervously, glancing down at the Queen Nefertitis beside her, pulsing like stars, and then looked up again as the last few lonely and solitary fireworks blazed briefly across the skyline behind me, lost against the mass of the strange city, searching silently for a home. And then she said yes.

*

At the Peacocks' now, Hyo-Sonn was a constant presence: in the kitchen, in the living room... at one point in the bathroom when I opened the door to take a shower, dusting the top of the medicine cabinet on a small stepladder. One morning when I returned to the Peacocks' apartment from Lydia's, I found to my complete bafflement that all the books on the living room shelves had been turned around so that the spines faced the walls and the pages faced the room. I checked in the library – the same thing had happened there. With slight trepidation, I opened my bedroom door and looked up at my own shelves – all my books had been turned inwards too.

"What's happened – what's happened with all the books?" I asked Rose Peacock that night, rather at a loss for how to approach the issue.

"It's Hyo-Sonn, you know," said Rose in an offhand manner. "She hates looking at the spines of books. Can't say I blame her!" she added, in case I was thinking of making any criticism of Hyo-Sonn for this. I wasn't – to be quite honest I wouldn't have known where to start. But unmistakeably a rather hostile atmosphere had now fallen over the table, and I suddenly felt it would probably be best if I went out for dinner that night.

I had noticed they had started keeping the study door closed almost constantly, even when they were at home, even when they were in there, and I felt nervous thinking about the print hidden behind the door, invisible, out of my control. Might the edges start to curl slightly inside the frame? How well did the Peacocks know the original painting, the colours used, the aluminium on the heart? How well did I? Perhaps the print was a less exact replica than it seemed? I felt we hadn't checked carefully enough. We shouldn't have had so much to drink before we swapped them. I kept finding excuses to ask the Peacocks to let me into the study, asking to borrow a book on south-east Asia or pretending to look at the pleasant view towards the Institute of Fine Arts on 78th Street or the sculptures on the sideboards, and while in there I would glance up apprehensively at the replacement print of 'The Weighing of the Heart' and try to see it as the Peacocks saw it, and on my third or fourth such attempt Marie snapped:

"What the hell are you going in the study all the time for?"

I hardly ever slept in my own room at the Peacocks' any more, preferring to stay at Lydia's, but I made an exception one night when Lydia was out for the evening with her friend Ana, and to my horror found myself sleepwalking in the most alarming fashion. Sleepwalking is something I've been prone to, unfortunately, since my early teens. If you've never done it, it's a peculiar thing: while you're in the sleepwalking state, although you're walking around, opening doors, picking things up and what have you, the logic of a dream applies utterly – so you might be searching for your grandfather's dog, for example, even though the dog died two decades ago on another continent, or you might be trying to find your wallet because the car's running low on petrol (I often used to find I was looking for something). It all makes perfect sense while you're still in the dreaming state. But as soon as you snap out of it – as soon as your girlfriend puts a concerned hand on your shoulder, or, more worryingly, as soon as some sense of real-world danger manages to intrude into your sleeping state (finding yourself opening a window often does it) you are instantly sent spinning back to normal, and the whole rationale for your nocturnal ramblings suddenly seems utterly crazy – a realisation that often provokes a curious feeling not unlike shame, in my experience. Anyway, the night that Lydia was out in the West Village with Ana I snapped out of my dream state to find myself in the dull, neon-tinged semi-darkness that is about as black as New York nights ever get, beside the wall of the Peacocks' study, half way through trying to clamber up on to their desk in order to grab 'The Weighing of the Heart' and remove it from the wall.

"Nick!" a woman's voice said sharply, and I swung around to find Marie Peacock standing in the study doorway in a long nightdress with the sisters' air rifle in her hands – the one Jeff had used to make all those holes in the hallway wall. "What the hell are you doing?" she asked.

I immediately began to snap out of my sleepwalking state, and one by one the groggy details of my dream came back to me: I had got out of bed and made my way into the study in order to check that the replacement print of 'The Weighing of the Heart' was still the one hanging in the frame there – in order to check the original hadn't come back. Of course, that made no sense at all now; how could it come back? Furthermore, I was aware that I was wearing only my boxer shorts. I shakily climbed down from the desk. Marie had still not lowered the air rifle.

"Young Nicholas," she said again. "What on earth is going on?" And I was sure I saw her flick a quick glance over my shoulder at the painting above me.

"I'm sorry," I said. "I – I sleepwalk, sometimes. I'm sorry – I'm sorry to have woken you."

"What the hell were you doing on the desk?" she asked.

"I..." I glanced at the desk, trying to convey the idea that I had barely been aware of its existence before that moment. "In my dream I was – I was climbing a tree," I said. "I was a child, back home in London. I was climbing a tree."

"Dreaming of climbing a tree..." repeated Marie, as if trying the idea out for size. She seemed to remember she was holding the air rifle then and silently lowered it at last. I took a deep breath and felt my heart rate begin its long journey back to normal.

"I used to live near a park," I continued. "When I was a child. There was a park – at the end of my street."

"Oh, for God's sake, go back to bed," she said brusquely, adding, half to herself: "We'll have to start locking the study at night if you carry on like this."

I trudged back to my room, but when I closed my bedroom door and got back into bed I felt certain

Marie was still out there in the hallway, staring up suspiciously at the painting. This sleepwalking was a worrying development, I thought; I was actually in serious danger of drawing attention to what we'd done. Perhaps I should always stay at Lydia's from now on, I thought, or lock myself in my bedroom if I stayed at the Peacocks'; perhaps Lydia and I ought to move out altogether.

*

Lydia quit her job, and began to spend her time either at home or at her studio in Hell's Kitchen working on her print for the Latza gallery, going through the exact colour matches the printers were proposing one by one and deciding on the size of the print and the style of the passe-partout. She bought a gold necklace showing a snake eating its own tail, the Egyptian symbol for eternity. It was beautiful and she looked beautiful wearing it, but how much did a thing like that cost? I didn't know. I was afraid to ask. I didn't want her to think I was suspicious. But I kept thinking about the fact that the painting had been worth three hundred thousand dollars; had she really got only a hundred for it? Of course, I knew I was just being silly, but the truth was that I just didn't know; she could easily have been given two hundred by Hector's friends, or four hundred, told me she had only got one and kept the rest herself. Or maybe she gave some of it to Hector. But the idea of my bringing any of this up was impossible.

I continued to have vivid dreams, and although as far as I knew there was no repeat of the sleepwalking incident, the episode had clearly unsettled me; the thing was that it reminded me a bit of something that had happened to me when I was little, when I was about eight years old.

I had come downstairs in the middle of the night one night having heard a noise to find a burglar in the back room, frozen, half in shadow, half illuminated by the weak moonlight, caught in the act of picking up the video recorder, and I remember thinking that it was appropriate that he was picking up the video recorder since he himself looked like he was on pause. He was looking right at me and I was looking right at him, and behind him I was conscious of a glint in one of the panes of glass beside the doorknob of the French windows, something that shouldn't have been there, something wrong. Perhaps that had been the noise I'd heard from upstairs, him breaking that pane of glass. Perhaps that was what had woken me up.

He looked at me, he kept looking at me, and then

slowly he put down the video recorder and stood up straight. At the time I remember I thought of him as being about my parents' age, but thinking about it now he was certainly much younger, maybe only in his early twenties, maybe even in his late teens. He looked scruffy; he had on a jacket that looked too thin for winter, and a dark woollen hat, and he was unshaven. He put the video down and looked at me.

"Close the door," he said almost silently. "The door, close the door. Slowly. Quietly."

I reached behind me and closed the door. He walked up to me then and knelt down so his face was level with mine. He said he was a friend of my mum and dad's. He said they'd borrowed some of his stuff and he had just come round to take it back home. But somehow he could see that I didn't believe that so he changed tack and pulled a short kitchen knife out from his inside jacket pocket and told me that if I made a noise he would cut my throat. He said my mum and dad were upstairs in bed and they couldn't help me. He said no one could help me. He said I was on my own.

He watched me for a minute, holding the knife, which gleamed along its blade where the moonlight slid through the gaps in the curtains, and then he gradually backed away towards the TV and video, still watching me, unplugged them, silently stacked them one on top of the other, picked them up, and backed his way out through the French windows. I stood there for a long time after he'd gone, and every minute or so the wind would catch one of the doors and flick it gently against the jamb. It began to rain a bit, and I could see raindrops start to speckle the carpet through the gap in the doors. At about seven o'clock I heard my parents begin to stir, and eventually they came downstairs for breakfast and found me.

I began to get nightmares after that, and in the end my parents felt they had to take me to the doctor. Sometimes it seemed like I could see the nightmares even when I was awake. Sometimes I seemed to black out. There were a few different doctors over the years, and what they always wanted to know was how the incident had made me feel. How it made me feel... I never knew how to answer them. But I remembered that idea he had mentioned; that no one could protect me. I remembered that feeling that I was on my own. I suppose I felt like I never wanted to put myself in that position again. I never wanted to be the victim.

I seem to have got rather distracted. I had been talking about my dreams following the sleepwalking incident. These dreams... they gradually became more and more frequent, and more and more lifelike. One night I dreamt there was a man in the bed, in between us, but when he rolled over to hug me it had been Lydia all along. One night I felt a cat crawl over my sleeping body, its claws sinking into my skin like needles, and woke up to find nothing there. One night I dreamt I was back home in London where the park started at the end of my street, surrounded on three sides by rangy teenagers looming in for the attack. Hector stepped in to help me, his shirt snapping in the wind like an American flag, and I said, "No, Hector, no, it's all right, I can handle this," but he knocked the kids to the ground for me, and I rushed upstairs to my childhood bedroom and looked in the mirror and mangled my face until it looked like his. One morning, leaving the building to set off for work, I noticed a little bird fluttering from branch to branch in the tree just beside our entrance awning. It was a pretty little thing, black with red and yellow patches on its wings, and it reminded me somehow of the ba I had thought I had seen in Horseheads. It sprang from the branch to the awning, and then leapt north towards the next building along, stopping for a moment in one of the trees there and turning its head back towards me almost as if it were trying to make sure it still had my attention. I walked towards it, and it moved up into the next tree north, and I followed it across 78th Street and past the Institute of Fine Arts to the corner of the next street, where it stopped in front of an apartment block almost identical to ours. I looked up at the building – many of the buildings along this stretch of Fifth Avenue were very similar, but this one really did seem to be a more or less exact duplicate – and then looked back to the ba, but it had gone, and just as I was about to head back towards the subway station and head off to work a young couple came out of the building's main entrance, followed by a real estate agent holding a brochure showing an elegant roof garden looking out over Central Park.

"And it's available immediately," she was telling the couple.

They all shook hands and exchanged thank-yous, and then the couple got into a cab and I stopped the realtor and said, "Is there an apartment for rent in this building?"

"Yes, sir," she said. "On the top floor, with access to a very attractive roof garden." She looked at her watch. "I've got an appointment in the West Village in half an hour, but I could take you up to see this place now for a minute or two if you're interested?"

We went up in the elevator and stopped at the top floor. Two doors faced us in the corridor.

"You'll share the roof garden with the people

who live in this apartment here," the realtor said, gesturing briefly. She unlocked the door to the apartment and we walked through the small hallway that led to the bedroom, just as it did in Lydia's flat. In fact, the apartment was identical: a living room/kitchen, whose windows faced 79th Street and whose door opened on to the roof garden, and a bedroom dominated as in Lydia's flat by a large, ornate double bed. After mentioning in passing and as quickly as possible the colossal rent, the realtor began to describe the view, and I followed her out through the kitchen to the roof garden, where we gazed across at the hornbeams and beech trees of Central Park and the blue-green pitched rooves of the Metropolitan Museum.

*

We had a rather nerve-wracking goodbye drink with the Peacock sisters before we moved out. Although unperturbed by the news that we were a couple, they seemed confused, even hurt, when we told them we were leaving, refusing to accept our stated explanation that we wanted to start again in a place of our own. Or perhaps that was just Rose. I had the distinct feeling that Marie was much less sorry to see us go.

"But you practically live together now," Rose was saying, tugging at her coat cuffs distractedly. "So difficult to get good tenants..."

"Where are you moving to?" asked Marie.

I glanced at Lydia. "Oh, you know, looking in the neighbourhood..." I said vaguely.

"We're going to stay with some friends of mine in Spanish Harlem for right now," Lydia improvised.

"Just until we get a place of our own," I said.

"Well," said Rose. "We must come visit once you're settled in. And you know you're always welcome to drop in on us." She turned to her sister. "They make a very handsome couple, don't they? I must say I'm very pleased for young Nicholas."

"He's done very well for himself," Marie agreed.

"I saw it coming, you know," said Rose.

"Well, I didn't!" said Marie gruffly. "Young Nicholas, if you'll permit a boxing metaphor, I'd say you're punching *well* above your weight!"

"Joking aside, come back and visit us any time," Rose said, looking from one to the other of us. "Or come to Water Mill one weekend with us. Of course, we rarely have room in the car, but there's always the Hampton Jitney!" (A rather overpriced bus service.)

"Well," I said awkwardly. "Thank you. And I have very much – enjoyed living here."

"You liked all our artwork and what not, didn't

you?" said Rose. "A little culture. Must have been nice. All the paintings. You were always peering at them all the time."

"Always wanting to see what we had in the study," said Marie, and I felt certain she was about to mention the sleepwalking incident, which I hadn't discussed with Lydia. But Rose interrupted her blithely with a complacent smile, saying, "The study? Young Nicholas, we keep that room locked for a reason! The Peacock crown jewels..." she added contentedly.

This phrase was presumably some sort of family shibboleth, as Marie immediately seemed to forget whatever train of thought she had been about to pursue, and said, "Ah, we were lucky..." going misty-eyed and clasping Rose's hand. "You bought a painting like some of those we have in that study back in the 60s, you could sit back and relax for the rest of your life... I mean it. And it was the same thing with real estate. It's your generation I feel sorry for," she continued. "Young people like yourselves. Young Jeffrey and his girlfriend, for instance. We've tried to guide them, we've given them some small sums to invest wisely. But at the same time you want a boy to stand on his own two feet, don't you..."

"Like you have, young Nicholas," put in Rose. "That's what we've always liked about you. You were unsatisfied with your lot, so you got up out of the gutter and you darn well changed things around. Left Ireland behind and didn't look back."

"England, dear," said Marie.

"England – of course. What did I say?" asked Rose.

"Ireland, dear. I dare say an Englishman would find that rather insulting."

"Yes," said Rose. "Apologies, young man."

"A bit like if someone mistook you for a Mexican..." continued Marie.

"Good God..." murmured her sister, visibly appalled.

Chapter 9

In the last days before we moved out, the Peacock sisters seemed to be arguing a lot; we could hear them sometimes above Lydia's flat or through the walls, but it was hard to make out what they were saying, and they always fell silent when they heard me enter their apartment. We said a formal goodbye in the lobby of the building, their handshakes somewhat stiff, and perhaps I was imagining it, but it seemed almost like neither of them wanted to look me in the eye. For the fifth or sixth time that day, for probably the hundredth time that week, I thought about the print of 'The Weighing of the Heart' upstairs in the study like a cuckoo in the nest. Perhaps now we were leaving I would at last be able to think about something else.

We moved our possessions into the new apartment and decorated it in much the same way Lydia's had been decorated, only with my artwork now side by side with hers on the walls. She placed her Egyptian cat figurines along the desk and set the torso of Tutankhamun up by the mirror and draped her jewellery around its neck and her eggshell-blue dress from its shoulders. We sat in the kitchen drinking coffee and out on the roof garden smoking just as we had at the Peacocks'. The apartment was exactly the same as Lydia's original flat, although to my surprise and disconcertment I found that I no longer had to duck my head when I went into the tiny bathroom. I stood nervously in front of the mirror. I couldn't be..? Was I getting *shorter*? Lydia came in and I quickly made as if I had been brushing my teeth. She began to organise her shampoos and lotions in the cabinet above the sink.

"What are all these pills?" she asked me, moving my things. "'Neurpraxin'. Do you take all of these different pills every day?"

"Not every day, no," I replied, and left the room.

"Hold on," she called after me. "What are they all for?"

"Asthma," I said.

She went to an auction at Doyle's and came back with some Queen Anne chairs, a Chippendale cabinet and some beautiful art nouveau lamps. "Wow," I said. "You must be really – you must be really burning through your share."

"Well..." she said. "That's what it's there for."

I stroked her back and it sounded like the sea at

night. I put my mouth wet on her neck like an animal's. I sat out on the roof and listened to the wind whistling in the slats of the wooden water towers on the rooves around me.

I bought a small blue statue of Bes, the protector of households, from the Brooklyn Museum of Art, and placed it in front of our front door in the lee of the doorframe, and I lined up my books on Egypt from the Ashmolean and the Met and carefully hung my painting of the ba returning to its tomb on the wall by the window and placed my framed sketch of the goddess Ma'at – the one that looked like Lydia – on the bedside table. Lydia sat on the bed and watched me, and asked me to tell her about how my interest in Ancient Egypt had begun. Was it back home in England? Had my parents encouraged it?

As I may have mentioned, I tend to dislike reminiscing, but she insisted, and almost without realising it, as she sat propped up against the pillows listening, I found myself back at the British Museum as a teenager, following an unruly crocodile of classmates in a long diagonal line across the enormous windswept museum forecourt, all of us dressed in our absurd identical white shirts and black ties, the traffic on the streets outside the museum's fearsome fence bumping and spitting like a wounded snake, as it always seemed to back then, and may still do today, for all I know. We passed through sheets of dust past Greek vases and Chinese ceramics, Victorian tea sets and Japanese mirrors, our teacher mumbling facts and anecdotes in an uninspired fashion, introducing us to the Egypt galleries with accounts of the fertile earth in the Nile Valley, the exact dimensions of the pyramids, and the distasteful details of how the Egyptians got the brains out of the skulls of their dead. Ornate, gilded sarcophagi ranged around us like sunbathers, and I was thinking about that bit in 'The Catcher in the Rye' when the little kids ask him where to find "them mummies in them toons" and simultaneously about the shapely behind of the girl a few feet ahead of me, whose name escapes me now, and whether she would be coming to that Saturday's party at the home of whoever's parents had been foolish enough to go away for the weekend.

There were too many of us in the gallery and some horseplay from the group of idiots next to me meant I got pushed to one side and found myself suddenly standing right up against a small glass case containing a tiny jade-coloured object set on a gold mount. The group began to move off into the other half of the room, but I stayed put, peering through the glass at this delicate little jewel that seemed to collect and draw in the light from the room around me. I read the explanatory label next to it, which said it was the 'heart scarab' of Pharaoh Sobekemsaf I and originated from Thebes in 1590BC. The label went on to explain that heart scarabs helped protect you at the moment of death, giving the full story – so familiar to me now – of the ostrich feather and the weighing scales, Anubis and the Devourer, and conjecturing that this particular scarab had been stolen by tomb-robbers in 1109BC. The label translated a spell that was inscribed on the scarab's base, in which the dead person begged his heart not to speak up against him at the moment of judgment: "Oh my heart, which I had from my mother, do not stand up as a witness against me, do not be opposed to me in the tribunal, do not be hostile to me in the presence of the Keeper of the Balance..."

I broke away from the school party soon after that, not an unusual occurrence in those days, I'm afraid, and left the museum to meander through the spokes of Covent Garden, black taxis jostling in the early-evening streets around me, narrow between the Edwardian four-storeys and the dusky glass fronts of the chain stores, the pedestrians overtaking the traffic, swamping it, the pitched battle of the Strand, buses mounting the pavement, cyclists shooting behind them, and a glimpse of the river flashing down every side street. I moved on to the tall, thin crush of Fleet Street, the secret legal alleyways, the monumental dome of St Paul's gleaming through coats of dirt. It was a habit of mine at that time to make these peripatetic journeys if I ever found myself alone in central London, an attempt to assuage some ill-defined dissatisfaction, I suppose, which more often than not ended up having the opposite effect. The rolling City tide was draining away around me into tube stations, buses and cabs, the shop shutters sliding shut like grimy metallic mouths and the pub doors swinging open to reveal rooms packed to the rafters like freight containers for animals on a rough ocean crossing, the creatures inside thrashing madly against the sides of the boxes, howls and puffs of breath escaping from the gaps where the planks don't meet. I pressed on, and caught sudden peeps of the single skyscraper the City could boast back then, its shoulder, its knee, its ugly black head. Window cleaners drifted up and down it as London sank into dusk around me, lights snapping on along the bending stripes of the streets, the Thames one way, the golden shimmer of Liverpool Street the other, and in the distance Centre Point, standing stark, grim and dutiful like a tombstone. In a deserted canyon street I leant against the wall of a law firm or a bank and unclenched my fist, and watched the jade scarab glow in my palm in the darkness.

I could feel the scarab in my wallet as I travelled

home on the commuter train that night, rustling through the brick vaults of Farringdon and Blackfriars, creeping stealthily towards the flatlands of south London. At London Bridge, the train rose up like a barge in a lock to float along on a level with the dirty rooftops, the rust and the graffiti, the jutting spires and the filthy window-frames, the rude tangle of rails and cables and street lights, the upper-floor doors of converted warehouses opening out on to nothing. Somewhere south of the track a small fire raged. I had had enough of it all.

We rolled in a lazy arc away from central London, and the solitary tower of Canary Wharf emerged slowly from the scrum of the skyline, a cold dagger glimmering under the black clouds. The first British settlers had fled to America from that spot, I recalled from my history lessons. Hard to imagine it, the pilgrims plunging headfirst into the elements, storms washing over them, pulling out from the dirty docks... the decrepit marshland a launch-pad for an unconquered continent.

In my school library I found an unloved-looking volume on the Ancient Egyptian 'Book of the Dead' published by the Dahesh Museum of Art in New York and slipped it into the enormous art portfolio case I was required to lug to and from school twice a week, and at home I would glance up from my drawings of the ba and the ka and my elaborate illustrations for the spells for repelling crocodiles and snakes and insects in my attic bedroom and watch the orange rooftops rising and falling around me and the church spires puncturing the grey skies, a lost kite drifting above the park, tarmac pouring down slopes in even lines, and in the back garden my bike chained up by its flat front tyre. From the street below came the sounds of cars accelerating with a crunch of gears as they left the bend in the road, the push and shove of the nearby supermarket, the warning sirens of lorries as they reversed to deliver beer barrels to local pubs, the whistling of burglar alarms and the sudden clumps of sound from birds or cats. At intervals the overland train to central London rattled thunderously across the iron bridge at the end of the street.

It was Sunday, and worshippers drifted aimlessly out of the nearby church, its uneven stones dyed black by petrol fumes, dirt whipping up from the pavement into their eyes as they submissively waited – as it seemed to my young and cynical eyes – for the working week to wash over them again like dirty water, to pull them down and hold them under until Friday, when they would breathlessly crawl free from the current and lie flat on the bank exhausted. And then on Monday it would start all over again. The tops of the tall trees waved to me dully in the wind, beckoning me, I felt with a shudder, and I looked away, at the high street past the bridge, where my reflection was always horribly familiar and at home in the barber's window, in the optician's and the record shop's, their low-watt signs flashing pathetically on and off, on and off, my feet splashing through potholed puddles in this empty, grey criss-cross of cold, flat, dismal streets. Clouds hung low and complete, enclosing the suburb like a huge white tent, and the mouths of the pubs seemed to call *bring out your dead*. I could have described it just as well with my eyes closed. I turned the pages of my book, and gripped my scarab in the heart of my hand. I would leave this behind, I promised myself. I would leave all this behind.

I still remember that final train journey from Paddington to the airport two or three years later. I had insisted on saying goodbye to my parents at the train station rather than at Heathrow, which didn't go down too well – but by then, they were used to what they regarded as my whims. Phone us as soon as you're at your halls of residence, they told me. We'll see you at Christmas. Remember to take all your medicine. I made whatever promises were required of me in order to board the train.

The carriage was full of matching yawns, business

travellers reaching for books or papers or rumpling up their clothes stuffing themselves into a corner of a seat to catch another few minutes of pre-airport sleep. Birds floated into their nests, tucked into the rooves above the top floors of the tower blocks west of the station as the train swam out between drainage pipes and deep, mildewed walls, through long terraces and tall blocks of flats, the railway depots and the parks, the high streets and the flyovers, freight-train cranes, warehouses, outskirt supercentres, the ring road, the river, the working week waking up at every station we tore through on the way. We whipped past a group of kids playing football on a tiny pitch encased in a cage, the ball bouncing off the wire mesh with a crash, washing flying like flags from the balconies of the brown housing block behind them. And then a control tower peeked over a hill, and a tailfin ran just above the rooves, ducking momentarily out of sight and then launching itself decisively upwards, gliding up and disappearing behind the fuzzy orange and white clouds decorated with shafts of light.

The plane was delayed, and delayed, and delayed again, and it was early evening before we were finally permitted to take our seats. I noticed I was biting a fingernail, something I hadn't done for years, something my mother always told me off for, and I took my hand away from my mouth and stared out through the layers of thick glass at the grey slab runway, at the white planes glittering under the floodlights in the sterile hum of the air conditioning.

The other passengers took their seats, some noisily, some quietly, and after that the lights went down, and then with a lurch, the plane forced itself into the air, shaking, shuddering and thundering as it rose, its metal panels straining against the natural order of things, and, as we banked, London lurched suddenly into view below us and I felt a sudden desire to look again at what I was leaving behind, just to make sure, the sea of orange lights, the snakes of grey roads, something moving fast like a rat – a helicopter, I realised suddenly – and the M25 like a river slipping through jungle as we moved away into the darkness, away from the shrinking glow. The air conditioning roared.

I didn't feel at all like trying to sleep, so I made a distracted attempt to read a book, the air conditioning roaring in my ears, and watched the tiny white plane on the seat-back screen inching its way across the black sea towards land. I willed it forward into the dark sky above Canada, and after a while, mine was the only seat still upright and the only light still lit as my fellow passengers slipped one by one into darkness. Despite myself I must have drifted off, because when I got up to go to the bathroom, I could now see out of the window orange dots marking the coast ahead, clusters of orange and white lights, rivers dragging in the sea to form lakes inland, and the moon, reflected in the water, running alongside the plane. I watched for a while at the porthole by the bathrooms, and the sea was an early-morning grey against the black horizon when my patience was finally rewarded with the orange ladders of a city grid, the white beads of a bridge strung across a dark ravine like a necklace, and the moon beginning to light up crevices in the landscape like a torch. Everything was as still and silent as a painting.

Clouds began to obscure my view, rolling black clouds that made it seem as if the plane were flying low over the water. But through the gaps, I saw boats coming into harbour, and other aeroplanes flashing in the sky. A stewardess asked me to sit down, and from my aisle seat I leaned over uncomfortably to follow the view, stretching my neck, and shortly afterwards there was a sickening lurch as the plane swung down to begin landing. Then, with a protracted rush of noise and a tremor and a bump, we slipped down on to the runway to a ripple of sleepy applause from my fellow passengers. I unclipped my seatbelt and leant towards the window and peered left and right until at last I saw poking up miles west the lit spires of the Empire State Building and the Chrysler Building, and to their left the vast wall of skyscrapers like a gateway in the harbour, the Twin Towers its two gigantic gateposts. I sat down again, rolling my scarab between my thumb and forefinger, watching it gleam in the light of this new world.

*

We were walking down Fifth Avenue one evening on our way to have dinner at the Frick Collection restaurant when I saw a silhouette I recognised instantly up ahead, coming towards us, a gait, a turn of the head. It was Hannah, and there was no way of avoiding her. She pressed on towards us, oblivious; beside me, holding my hand, Lydia continued to talk enthusiastically about her day working with the printers at the gallery. And then Hannah saw me, and she stopped still and began to shake and shout.

"Don't come near me, you bastard!" she shouted. "Don't come any nearer!"

Lydia was looking at me, her eyes wide in alarm. We stopped where we were. Hannah continued to stare at me, shouting, blazing with rage.

"Don't come near me!" She was shaking. And

then abruptly, as if she had just at that moment realised it was in her power to do so, she ran off.

Lydia was very upset. We sat down on a bench by the wall to the park as the traffic snarled and growled around us. "Who was that? Was that Hannah?" she asked. "Why is she so angry? What did you do?"

"I don't know," I said. "I didn't do anything. I didn't think – I didn't think she would still be so upset. It's been months now since – since we broke up. I didn't think she'd still be so upset."

"She seemed very upset," said Lydia. "I thought you said the break-up – I thought you said it went okay."

"It was... I thought it did," I said. "I really don't know what's the matter with her."

"Maybe you should get in touch," Lydia suggested. "Not now, but... maybe in a few days you should get in touch. Email her. See if you can find out what's wrong. I mean she's obviously – She seemed very angry."

"Yes," I said. "Yes, that's a good idea. I'll do that. I'll email her."

Lydia was looking at me strangely. "You told me it went okay," she said.

*

Lydia's birthday was coming up that Saturday and for her present, I was planning to give her the first painting I had managed to finish for some time. It was an image of four wild geese being released to the four corners of the sky, a traditional Egyptian ceremony held to mark the accession of the new pharaoh. I'd been working on the painting without telling her at my studio space in Bushwick and now it was wrapped up in a box under the table beside her bed, and I was going to give it to her over breakfast on her birthday. We were just lying in bed fast asleep that morning when the buzzer rang. Lydia reached out for the intercom phone. It was the doorman.

"Ms Reis," he said. "There's a parcel down here for you. It's too big for your mailbox. I'm not sure where I should put it."

"Oh," said Lydia woozily. "Could you just hold on to it down there in your office for now?"

We didn't really know the doorman yet and he didn't sound very happy with that idea. "I could bring it up," he suggested grudgingly.

"That's very nice of you," she said. "I would really appreciate that. Thanks very much."

She got out of bed and stretched her arms out in a yawn, and moved over to the closet to put on her robe. A few minutes later, there was a knock at the front door and she padded out through the hallway to answer it. She came back with a large tube-shaped parcel and got back into bed to open it.

"What is it?" I asked.

She was unwrapping it. "Oh," she said slowly. "It's from Hector."

It was a replica of the giant obelisk known as 'Cleopatra's Needle' that stands in Central Park – or perhaps (equally fitting) the one on the north bank of the Thames. She silently let go of the parcel, half-unwrapped, and lay back down, pulling the duvet up around her shoulders. The present lay forlornly between us in the middle of the bed. I turned over with a sigh and tried to go back to sleep.

*

The next evening when the elevator doors opened, we were startled to see the Peacock sisters in the hallway, waiting in front of the door to the adjacent apartment.

"What are you two doing here?" Marie asked us, clearly as surprised as we were.

"Well, this is where we... this is where we moved to," I said.

"Here?" asked Rose, looking around superfluously. "We thought Spanish Harlem. Why didn't you tell us?"

"Tell you what?" asked Lydia politely.

"Why, that you moved in next door to young Vivian!" replied Rose. At that moment, the door to the apartment next to ours opened with a jolt and a young woman emerged who closely resembled Jeff's sister Annabel. She hopped up to her aunts and gave them each a peck on the cheek, saying, "Hi there, you two!" We let ourselves into our flat in silence and spent the evening trying not to think about it.

One night later that week, I came home to find Lydia sitting in the kitchen, her hands clasped around a half-drunk cup of coffee. She stood up immediately when I came in.

"Oh," she said. "Hello. I was... How are you?"

"I'm okay," I said. "How are you? What have you been up to today?" In the sink was another coffee cup, this one empty. "Have you had friends round?" I asked.

"Oh," she said again, getting up from the table. "Yes. Hector. Hector came round."

"Hector?" I said, startled. "Why?"

She turned away from me and opened the door to the roof garden. I followed her outside as she sat down on one of the garden chairs facing the park and nervously lit a cigarette from a pack that she or I must have left under the legs of the chair. It was a beautifully sunny evening and across the wide span of the park we could see hundreds, perhaps even thousands, of sunbathers sprinkled across the green lawns like confetti.

"Lydia," I said. "Why was he – why was he here?"

"It's okay, Nick," she said, a little impatiently. "It's okay. You know, I called him to tell him I'd moved out from the Peacocks' place, to tell him I'd moved in here – with you. You know, I wanted to tell him that. And – and quite naturally, he asked if he could come see the place. So, why not? There's no problem for him to come see the place, is there?"

"No," I said tentatively, sitting down on the chair beside her. "I guess not. Well, what did he – what did he think?"

She paused for a moment, and when I glanced around she seemed distressed or worried in some way, but as soon as she saw I was looking at her she collected herself and went on speaking. "He just said it looks like the old place."

"Well," I said. "Yes."

"Yes..." she said, and unmistakeably now there was something heavy and troubled in her tone.

"Are you all right?" I said.

She dragged on her cigarette, remembered me now and offered me one too, and said, "Yes, yes, of course. Yes, of course."

"So – you told him – you told him we live here?"

I asked.

She nodded.

"And you told him – we're engaged?"

She was quiet. "I – No," she said in the end. "No – you know... It was hard for him to hear we'd moved in together. It's hard for him, Nick. One step at a time, you know?"

I stood up. "Come on," I said. "Hard for him? What's so hard? You broke up. It happens. It was almost a year ago. People break up. You've met someone else now. He'll meet someone else."

"Nick..." she said. "Come on... You know life's not so easy like that. You know that. Yes, we broke up. All right. He knows that. But it's hard for him to take it that I've got a new boyfriend now. It's hard for him. We went through a lot together."

"What do you mean, went through a lot?" I asked.

"We went through a lot. We were married."

"Okay, but it's over now," I said insistently. "You've moved on. He needs to move on too."

"Nick..." she said. "It's not like a job. You know? It's not like – it's not like an old car. This relationship was a very important part of both our lives for a long, long time – for six years. We wanted –" She paused, and then continued: "We wanted to have a baby together. You can't just forget these things in a day.

You can't just wipe the slate clean."

"You wanted to have..." I said. "What do you mean? Why didn't – what – what happened?"

She was quiet for a long time then, wrapping her hair around her fingertips and looking down at the little brickwork wall that ran along the edge of the roof, just as it had at the Peacocks' place.

"We decided to try to have a baby," she said in the end. "And we tried, and we couldn't, and we – we went to the doctor, and we both had all the tests, you know, and – and it was him, he couldn't have children, and I – you know – I – it was okay, you know, we could adopt. I told him we could adopt, we could adopt if he couldn't have children. There are lots of children in the world that need – that need adopting. But to him – you know – his whole self-image, masculinity, whatever, and he changed, he really changed; it was like he wasn't the same man any more. And we grew apart," she said simply. "We grew apart..." She was crying now. I reached a hand out and stroked her shoulder.

"I used to hear her all the time, you know," she said suddenly, "in the old apartment. We had talked about her so much it was like she was real. Before we found out we couldn't have her. We used to joke that the Peacocks would move to Water Mill for good and leave us their apartment. We used to talk about her playing in the apartment and which room would be hers. And after – after we found out we couldn't have her, sometimes I would imagine I could hear her, up there, running from room to room, knocking things down, closing doors, knocking down piles of whatever, books, videotapes, all those things piled up that the Peacocks had everywhere all over the apartment. I never told him. And things were collapsing between us and I began to think that if he moved out that I would stop – that I would stop hearing her. And I did hear her less, once he'd gone. I did. But I was so glad when you moved in. Because if I ever heard noises from the apartment after that I could tell myself it was just you."

I put my arms around her and held her and kissed her hair, and after a long time like that I brought her inside and I held her on the bed until she fell asleep, and then I lay there thinking about her and Hector, and everything he knew about her, and everything he knew about us.

*

She let the lease on her studio space in Hell's Kitchen lapse and began spending most of her time at the Latza working on her print, usually arriving mid-morning and leaving with me at around six when I finished my shift. Samuel Latza had given her a dedicated space in the studio at the back. One day I walked in there and was startled to find her sitting deep in conversation with Martin Samarkos.

"Hello, Nick!" Samarkos said happily, breaking off to stand up and shake my hand.

"Hello," I said, looking at Lydia. "I didn't know you two knew each other."

She was wearing a tight grey dress that shone like an artwork I'd seen once that had tried to simulate moonlight.

"We just met," said Martin. "You know, I had dinner with Sammy the other night" – he meant Samuel Latza, and nobody called him Sammy – "and he told me about this fantastic artist who was coming in with a new print. He told me all about it (Ancient *Egypt*...) and I thought it sounded like just my thing, so he asked me to come take a look at the proofs, and once I'd seen them I knew I *had* to collaborate with her."

"Collaborate?" I asked.

"Well, it's an idea Martin had," began Lydia apologetically.

"It's a fantastic idea!" said Martin. "I can see it now," he said to me. "I'm thinking she recreates her image as a route on a GPS screen which we project on to the wall of the gallery, and then I graffiti

Egyptian hieroglyphics all over it with spray-cans, using a number of different day-glo colours... I'm talking about a real Andy Warhol-Jean-Michel Basquiat clash of cultures, but for the iPhone generation..."

From the gallery, I could hear the sound of Samuel Latza arriving and being talked through the day's sales. One of my colleagues put her head around the door and asked if Lydia could come through for a second. Martin watched her with undisguised covetousness as she made her way across the room.

"Has she agreed to this?" I asked him as the door shut behind her.

"She will," he said. He was leafing through a contacts book.

"What are you doing now?" I asked, irritated.

"Consultancy I use. Have people heard of Queen Nefertiti? I'm thinking it might be better to base something around the old Boris Karloff Mummy."

"Consultancy?" I asked.

"Nick, Nick, Nick, you have got to chill out, my buddy," he said, thumbing through the address book. "Come on. This is the twenty-first century. Art is a conversation – like everything else. It's a two-way street. It's okay to ask people what they want."

"Ask people?" I said, finding myself speaking too

loudly. But I couldn't stop. "Did Picasso ask people if they wanted Guernica? Did Marcel Duchamp ask them if they wanted Fountain?"

He looked up at me, his face open and credulous, genuinely mystified, and then suddenly he started laughing, and carried on for a long time.

"Marcel Du*champ*... Nick, I've got to tell you," he said, "I don't want to hurt your feelings, but... that kind of attitude is exactly the reason why you're working in this gallery and I'm on the walls. Are you sleeping with this chick?"

"She's my fiancée," I said firmly.

"Okay," he said. "I'll give you that. It's not all bad in Nick World. Impressed." My colleague reappeared and asked if Martin could come through too, and he left the studio, giving me a short mock-bow at the door. "In fact, I take it all back. Dark horse, my buddy... There's *something* going on in there, anyway," he added, pointing at my forehead.

I sat down at the workbench and fumed, and that night as the cab drove us home I asked her, "What are you doing? What is this project with Martin Samarkos?"

"Nick," she said. "Come on. He's well-known, he's well-connected, and he's interested in collaborating with me. This could really help me."

"But he's terrible!" I said.

"I know," she said, putting her hand on mine. "I know he's terrible. But we don't have to follow his ideas. This GPS thing..." She smiled tolerantly. "You know, maybe I can persuade him to do something really good. I just think it's worth exploring. You never know. This could be a real chance for me."

"So are you going to do it?" I said sulkily.

"I don't know yet," she said, her voice hardening a little. "We're just talking. We're just talking about some ideas. It's okay if I talk to him about that, isn't it?"

She turned to look at me, but I didn't reply. I was looking out through the taxi's tinted windows, watching the frenzied streets swish by with a sudden sense of growing dread.

That night I dreamt we were sleeping in a huge, empty building, high on some towering, vertiginous upper floor. She was wearing an eggshell-blue dress and her hair was in pigtails. I had brought her there, I knew that – it was my idea to be there. But I woke up with the sudden knowledge that a tsunami was coming, and we rushed out of the room just in time to see it roaring towards us through the plate-glass windows. I held her tightly as the water hit and the building turned on its side in an agonising three-stage lurch; I tried to protect her head as we were buffeted around inside. Eventually, the building began bobbing lightly on the water like an enormous dinghy, and I crawled along the walls of the room we had been sleeping in as the water drained away, and I looked around for her, but she had completely disappeared. I searched for her for a long time, but I couldn't find her, and eventually I made my way to a fire-escape door, opening it to find myself at what was now the building's highest point, looking out forlornly over the flooded fields of the England of my youth.

*

I ran into Severin one night on my way home. She was in a restaurant in Chinatown just off Canal Street eating dinner with some friends and she motioned frantically through the window for me to come and join them.

"Hi," I said cautiously. "How are you?"

"Have you eaten? Come and eat. It's good," she said, turning a chair around from another table for me. I wasn't eager, but the waiter brought me some green tea and I sat down. "So what's going on with the Peacock sisters?" Severin asked.

I explained that I had moved out.

"I know that," she said. "I mean: something's going on with the Peacock sisters. Jeff got a call to go up and see them last night. They sounded really upset, you know? Especially Marie. He went up there, and he ended up staying overnight in the end, texted me saying he would tell me what was happening this evening. He had to stay there overnight because they were still waiting for the police to come."

"The police?" I said, the teacup suddenly hot in my hand.

"Yeah, something, I don't know," she said, trying to pick up a prawn with her chopsticks. "What are you doing?" she asked as I pushed my chair away from the table.

"I've got to go," I said. "Sorry. Thanks for the tea."

I rushed to the subway and when I got out on the Upper East Side I hurried along 77th Street until I was right in front of the Peacocks' building. I stood on the corner on the other side of Fifth Avenue and looked powerlessly up at it in all its impregnable robber-baron glory. I wished I had kept a set of keys. I wished I was able to find out somehow what was going on in there. I pictured the frame of 'The Weighing of the Heart' propped up by the sofa, the back dismantled, the print beside it on the carpet. Did they know? Did they know?

A police car shot past and I involuntarily took a

step back towards the park – and as I did so I glanced towards the café on the corner, and to my surprise spotted the Peacock sisters sipping fretfully from coffee mugs in the window.

I peered closer. It was definitely them. But this wasn't like them, drinking coffee in a coffee shop instead of just having a cup for free in their own kitchen. I crossed Fifth Avenue and moved cautiously towards the café. The sisters looked worn out, worried, their conversation intense. As I watched, the waitress came and brought them the bill, and Marie scrabbled in her purse for some cash, the notes swirling around like a small tornado before settling on the tray, and then they both stood up, pulling their jackets on, and, worried that they would see me, I backed away into 77th Street and then quickly headed north towards home.

*

I was beginning to feel tired and nervy and jumpy and upset. One day, I saw Hector's face in the background of a photograph. One day, I looked through a keyhole in our apartment and thought I saw an eye staring back, swirling, endless and deep, like the Milky Way, and I came away with a headache that forced me to lie down for the rest of the afternoon.

Sometimes, as we lay in bed or sat at the kitchen table, there was a thick silence that neither of us could read.

Her phone rang in the middle of the night one night, and we both sprang awake. It was the alarm – it had been set to the wrong time. We drifted back to sleep with difficulty. Almost as soon as we had done so, it went off again.

I looked out at the park from the flat roof, and watched a tall man with a small head clamber quickly over the wall and disappear into the shrubbery. I leaned against the gallery wall, taking a break from heaving some enormous eyesore of a canvas from one end of the space to the other, and saw Lydia and Samuel Latza laughing and smoking outside. A skateboarder rattled past, wheels heavy and rhythmic as a train. I had that strange feeling again like the building was rocking, like I was on a ship or in an earthquake. Did I mention that before? Waking in the morning, at the window I could make out tiny eyes. But it was probably just my ba.

The wind shook the window frames, and tree branches scraped across the glass. I ran my hands over the corner of the table, where there seemed to be some sort of bite mark; I tried to tell Lydia about it but she looked at me apprehensively and told me I must have just banged a piece of furniture into it or something like that. I caught a glimpse of somebody in jeans and a red and black zip-up jacket running into the park and through the trees but I stared and stared at the trees waiting for his tiny head to reappear but it never emerged.

I ran out of medicine and couldn't seem to make the time to get over to Brooklyn to pick up any more. I looked up at our apartment from the park one evening when I was returning from work and I knew Lydia was still at the gallery. There was a hint of slight activity up there and I started forward on one foot, but it was nothing, just the reflection of a plane going past, and I stepped back into my original position.

I watered our plants, and their leaves had grown so big they were almost frightening. I woke up in the night and for a moment, I was not sure whether I was next to Lydia or somebody else. I pulled the cover off her and looked at her naked body in my half-sleeping state. In my dream-logic, I realised they were both the same person.

I walked out into the street and a solid block of rain slammed into my face like a door.

I left work one evening and was walking to the subway when I saw Samuel Latza sitting eating with two older ladies in the restaurant next to Bogardus

Garden. I recognised the women he was with; of course I did. It was the Peacocks. Latza was listening intently to whatever it was they were saying; at one point he shook his head sadly and sympathetically like a great bull elephant. I hurried past them and down into the subway. On the train was a girl who looked like Lydia. To be honest I was seeing her everywhere. Once I even saw a double of myself with a double of her – those two I followed around a street corner and under the approach to the Manhattan Bridge, at which point they disappeared.

I ran into Severin one evening in a restaurant in Chinatown just off Canal Street. She was eating dinner with some friends and motioned eagerly that I should come and join them.

"Hi," I said. "How are you?"

"Have you eaten? Come and eat. It's good," she said, turning a chair around from another table for me. I was less than enthusiastic, but the waiter brought me some green tea and I sat down. "So what's going on with the Peacock sisters?" she asked.

I explained that I had moved out. "I know that," she said. "I mean: something's going on with the Peacock sisters. Jeff got a call to go up and see them last night. They sounded really upset, you know? Especially Marie. He went up there, and he ended up staying there overnight in the end, texted me saying he would tell me what was happening tonight. He had to stay overnight because they were still waiting for the police to come."

"The police?" I said, feeling a headache begin to clasp my forehead like a claw. I stood up as quickly as I could and headed out of the restaurant.

That night I turned into the Neue Galerie to get some dinner at Sabarsky's when there at a table by the newspaper rack I saw Marie Peacock with Hector. "May I take your coat, sir?" the waiter was saying to me. But I had already involuntarily backed away from the door.

"No, no, no thank you," I said, not taking my eyes off them. They were facing one another, deep in conversation. What were they doing together? What were they talking about? Had he told her about the painting?

Marie was asking Hector something, really quite frantically, and Hector kept looking away, as if reluctant to meet her gaze, his fingers working away at his collar. I left the restaurant and crossed the street, and then I waited and followed them at a distance when they came out on to the street some time later. It was just beginning to get dark, but they headed haltingly across Fifth Avenue and into the park, walking slowly, presumably keeping to Marie's pace. From there they made their way around the back of the Metropolitan Museum and gradually south until they were about level with 77th Street, the Peacocks' block. I stayed some way back from them, ducking behind the foliage so they couldn't see me. They stopped and stared up across Fifth then, straight towards the Peacocks' building. Marie seemed angry all of a sudden, and Hector, abandoning his earlier diffidence, joined in with a rant of his own. Then Marie pointed north, towards the building where Lydia and I now lived. There was a moment's silence, and then Hector nodded to her respectfully and they moved off in two separate directions, Marie towards home, Hector back into the park.

I decided to follow Hector. He walked up by the reservoir, idling near the edge. It would be so easy to push him in, drown him, I found myself thinking – except it wouldn't; he was much taller than me, especially lately. He walked around the circumference of the reservoir, clearly musing over something. He sat for a while at a bench gazing out at the lake, and then suddenly patted his pockets as a phone call came through, and stood and paced while he talked on the phone. It was strange seeing him up close. He was older than I had realised – maybe around forty – and his brown, handsome face was beginning to become marked by age, his eyes weathered and serious, his forehead etched with grooves. This idea I'd had that his head was too small... it looked perfectly normal.

I thought back to that night when he had visited Lydia's apartment and she had told him about the painting, remembered him sitting drinking beer at the kitchen table, confident and in control. I wished it was still lying there under our bed as we had sex above it. I wished we had never sold it, never handed it over to Hector and allowed him back into the heart of our lives. And what was he doing now, with Marie Peacock? What had he told her? He wanted me gone, I knew that much. He would do anything to get rid of me.

I could hear him talking, although I couldn't quite make out what he was saying. He had a clear New York accent; it was nothing like Lydia's. He had been born in America, I recalled; it was his parents who were Portuguese. I heard Lydia's voice in my mind: "We went through a lot... We wanted to have a baby."

He finished his phone call and put his phone back in his pocket, and then headed out of the park at about 96th Street and up into El Barrio. I continued to follow him.

The atmosphere in the streets changed instantly as soon as we left the borders of the Upper East Side.

The buildings were suddenly run down, paint peeling, awnings torn, flecks of palimpsest-like posters flickering free in the breeze, Puerto Rican flags flying from rusty fire escapes, a group of young men leaning against a chain-link fence. I felt out of place – even, perhaps, in danger. Unexpectedly, at one point, the street curved sharply upwards to form an enormously steep hill, so unusual for Manhattan, and we trekked up it almost panting as the cars and buses struggled beside us, gears grinding painfully in protest. The last shadows of the day loomed over potholes and laundromats as we rounded a corner, and I hung back a little while Hector entered a worn-out Mexican grocery store and then a couple of minutes later emerged from the gloom of the doorway unwrapping a packet of cigarettes. He stood on the street corner lighting one, and from the building opposite, a decaying chunk of grey brickwork cut crudely into the hill, a woman came out and waved and said, "How you doing, Hector!" and Hector smiled and raised a hand in greeting.

Was his block, then? I looked around down the long, straight streets, at the low-rise schools and churches and the cheap Chinese restaurants and barbershops, at the corrugated iron of closed-down shops, at the last red rays of the sun creeping across the walls and rooftops like the tide going out along the shore. And then he looked up and saw me.

Chapter 10

Lydia was reading on the bed when I got back home, and I opened the door somewhat shakily and sat down on the chair by the desk.

"What's wrong?" she asked, putting her book down. "Nick? Are you all right? You look very pale."

"I'm okay," I said.

"What's wrong? Where have you been?"

"I've been –" I put my head in my hands and exhaled. "I'll tell you what happened," I said, looking up again. I exhaled again. "Oh... Well, let me start at the... I was just going to get something to eat at Sabarsky's, and I saw – I saw Marie Peacock having dinner there with – with Hector."

"With Hector?" she said. "They were in Sabarsky's?"

"Yes," I said. "I went in for something to eat, and – and they were there having dinner together."

"Okay..." she said. "You know, we've talked about how they're friends, right? Haven't we? I did tell you that. I told you they do business together from time to time – property," she said.

"Right," I said.

"I think they're working on something together at the moment," she said.

"Working on something?" I asked.

"Yes, Hector told me about it the other day," she said. "The Peacocks want to buy part of an apartment block on Fifth Avenue a few blocks north of here. Apparently, there've been a lot of problems with the sale, and some of the tenants are campaigning against it. East Meadow Building Against The Buyout; they've organised themselves."

"Okay," I said.

"One guy was even... Hector said Marie actually had to call the police about one guy last week; he was following her home, harassing her. Rose thinks they should pull out of the deal. She's never been in favour of it, that's what Hector said."

"Right," I said. "Okay."

"So what happened?" she asked. "Did you speak to them, or – or what..?"

"No... I was – I was worried about why they were together," I said.

"Worried?" she said. "What do you mean, worried?"

"Well..." I said nervously. "I'll tell you... You see, when they left I followed them into the park –"

"You followed them?" she said.

"To see what they were – you see, I was worried about what they were talking about. And then, when Marie left, Hector went up into El Barrio –"

"What? You followed him?" she said. She got up from the bed. "You followed him home?"

"Not home, but – yes, because I was worried about what they were doing," I said impatiently. "Had he told them about the painting? Had he told them about the painting? I was worried about why they were together. But then when we got up into El Barrio he saw me," I continued. "He recognised me and he said – he said he wanted to talk to me."

"Wait a minute, wait a minute. What do you mean, he wanted to talk to you?"

"That's what he said. He said he wanted to talk to me. He said he'd been meaning to talk to me. He'd been meaning to come down to the gallery one day when you weren't there and talk to me."

She was watching me silently. I wasn't sure what she was thinking. "What about?" she said quietly in the end.

I took a deep breath. "Look, Lydia, I know he means a lot to you," I said, trying to choose my words carefully. "I know – I know you were very close, the two of you. But – so I'm just going to tell you what he said. I'm sorry if it – but this is what he said. He told me he wanted me to leave you, that he wanted me to break it off with you and move out of this apartment. And he told me that if I didn't do that then he would tell the Peacocks that I stole their painting."

She looked away from me, down at the floor. "Nick, did this really..?" she said quietly. "Nick, is this – is this really true?"

"It is," I said insistently. "It is true. He told me not to tell you. He said if you found out and you asked him about it he would deny it, he would just deny it."

"Oh God," she said, still not looking at me. "Nick, you know, even if he did say this to you, he can't mean it, he can't possibly mean it. I mean, how could he tell the Peacocks? He was just as involved in it as we were."

"I don't know. I don't know, but you didn't see him, Lydia. He meant it. He's trying to break us up; that's what he wants. He wants you back... He's trying to break us up, so he can get you back."

Lydia put her head in her hands. "Oh, God..." she said. "Look, maybe he does still... I mean, it's understandable, Nick. It's understandable. It was an important relationship for us both." She looked up. Her eyes were wet with tears. "Let me just talk to him, Nick. He won't do this. He really won't."

"Lydia, he will do this," I said. "He wanted me to – he *told* me – to let you down gently. That's what he said." She looked across at me when I said that. "He told me to take my share of the money and just go, go away, leave New York, go somewhere... I don't know where he wanted me to go. But we've got to act first," I said. "We've got to do this quickly, before he realises I'm not going to leave and goes to tell them."

Lydia stared at me, confused. "Do what?" she asked.

"We've got no other choice," I said. "All we can do is tell the Peacocks first, tell them it was him."

"Tell them it was him?" she repeated, uncomprehending. "But – but they'll call the police."

"That's what *he* wants for *me!*" I shouted. In the mirror, I could see my ba beating its wings furiously, wheeling in a circle around the bedroom. "That's what he wants to happen to me! Is that what you want? Is that what you want to happen?"

"No! No!" she said, crying openly now. "Of course not. But we can't tell them it was him – they'll call the police, they'll arrest him."

I sat down in front of her, calmer now, and took her hands. My ba settled on the dresser behind her. "Lydia," I said. "We've got no other choice."

"I can talk to him," she said desperately.

"No, Lydia," I said. "You know what he thinks about us. You've said it yourself. When he came round here the other day, you wanted to tell him we were engaged, but you couldn't – because he can't face it. You told me that. You know how he feels. What could you possibly tell him? The only thing that would satisfy him is if we break up."

"Oh, God..." she said.

"You know it is. He wants me gone. This is what he wants to do. How can you talk him out of this? You can't talk him out of loving you. He loves you."

"Oh, God..." she moaned. I stroked her hair. She laid her head against my lap and sobbed, deep, wracking sobs that convulsed her body. My ba was gazing calmly at me from the top of the wardrobe.

"Let's go over to the Peacocks' now," I said. "While we still have time."

*

The Peacocks sat us down in the study and fussed over us to an uncommon degree, bringing us tea and coffee and offering us cookies from an ancient-looking glass jar. I think they could see that Lydia was upset and they were worried about her. Eventually they sat down on the settee facing us and waited politely for us to tell them whatever it was that was evidently on our minds. The print of 'The Weighing of the Heart' hung in its heavy frame behind them, Anubis carefully setting the scales, Thoth preparing his long reed brush, the Devourer squat and hungry at their heels.

I took a sip of tea, unsure how to begin. I had realised on the way over that I had no plausible way of explaining why Hector would have trusted me with this information. Perhaps I could say I couldn't tell them – perhaps I could say it would mean breaking a confidence. That might appeal to their old-fashioned sense of honour. I hoped they wouldn't question me too closely.

Marie cleared her throat, and I forced myself to begin.

"I've –" I said awkwardly. "I've got some – some very bad news. And I'm sorry to have to tell it to you, erm, like this."

"What is it?" Marie asked, concerned, leaning forward. Beside me, Lydia was sitting in total silence, looking down at the floor.

"I'm so sorry to tell you this," I said, "but Hector –"

I broke off.

"What is it?" asked Marie again, more forcefully this time. "Come on, young Nicholas, spit it out, for

God's sake."

Beside me, Lydia had silently begun to cry.

"Your painting," I said, looking up at 'The Weighing of the Heart.' "Your painting..." But through the glass I had caught the Devourer's eye somehow. It blinked, slowly, and gradually and implacably turned its scaly head towards me. I looked away, and made myself continue. "Hector – stole it," I said.

"Hector what?" asked Rose.

"He stole your painting," I said, the words coming out in a rush now. "He stole it. He stole it and he sold it."

"What painting? Which painting?" asked Marie, looking around the room.

"Hector? Hector Soares?" asked Rose. "Lydia's Hector?"

"He's not –!" I began angrily, and then calmed myself down. "He stole your painting," I said slowly. "'The Weighing of the Heart.' The Edward Hazlemere painting. 'The Weighing of the Heart.'" They both looked up at the frame above their heads.

"Nicholas," said Marie. "It's right here."

"Take it out of the frame," I said. "Look at it. It's gone. It's not the painting in there. It's not the painting. It's just a poster. He's taken the painting. He's sold it."

Marie stood up, Rose shortly after. I stood up too. "I don't –" said Marie.

I moved forward and reached out for the picture frame and began to pull it down off the wall, making sure to smear my fingerprints firmly on the glass, on the backing board, on the four wooden sides of the frame. Marie grabbed the other side, with surprising force and for a moment we struggled for control of it. Then we reached a sort of alignment, and together we laid the frame carefully on the desk.

The back was exactly as I remembered it. I pulled at the nails with my fingers, but Marie barked, "Rose. Get a hammer," and when her sister returned Marie flipped the nails out with the back of the hammerhead. We pulled the backing board off the frame, and I made sure to plant my hand right on the back of the print as it came free and began to slowly roll itself up.

"Well, I'll be damned," said Marie quietly. She pulled the print out of my grasp and glanced up at me, and then looked down again at the print. "Well, I'll be damned," she said again. "Rose. Rose. This is a fucking poster." She sat down at the desk, pressing the print out flat with her hands, placing coasters at the corners to hold it down. The baboon on the top of the scales leapt quickly out of her way as her hands swept by, and then settled back into position.

Rose joined her at the desk, standing at her elbow. I leant awkwardly beside the wall, feeling suddenly rather short of breath.

"Hector did this?" asked Marie, turning to look at me. "Hector Soares?"

"I'm sorry," I said.

Marie turned her gaze to Lydia, who was still sitting mutely on the sofa, staring at a spot on the floor by her feet.

"Lydia..." said Marie softly. "Hector?"

There was a moment of perfect silence, broken only by the rattle of china as my ba flew down from the curtain rail and perched itself on the lip of my teacup.

Slowly, without looking up, Lydia nodded.

"My God," said Marie, turning to Rose. "My God." She looked over at the empty frame, leaning against the wall.

"You trust somebody..." said Rose, shaking her head.

"You do indeed," Marie replied. "You do indeed. And how did you – how did you find out?" she asked me.

"I –" I swallowed, my throat dry. "He told me," I said with difficulty. "He wants me to leave Lydia. He wanted to prove to me that – that he was dangerous. That he knew dangerous people. So he told me that

210

he'd stolen it and about – and about the people he'd sold it to."

As soon as I mentioned that Hector wanted me to leave Lydia, I saw Marie flick a glance at Rose, who pressed her lips together in a gesture of recognition or concurrence or agreement. Marie sighed heavily, as if something painful had to be admitted. But then she looked back at me, her eyes narrowing. "Dangerous?" she asked.

"He is a passionate man," Rose said quietly, and after a beat this seemed to satisfy her sister.

"Well, I suppose we had better call the police," said Marie sadly.

"I think so," I said, trying for the same tone of voice. I perched on the arm of the sofa beside Lydia and put my hand on her knee. "Lydia," I said. "We'd better go, I think."

Marie looked over at me. "No, no," she said. "You stay where you are, young Nicholas. You're exactly the one they'll need to talk to." She stood up. "Rose, you keep the two of them company for a minute. I'll just go and telephone from the other room."

Marie left the study, the door clicking behind her with a sound almost like a key turning in a lock. I sat back down on the settee. Rose sat down silently at the desk. It almost felt like she was guarding us.

Marie returned after a few minutes. "I told them

everything you said. I told them – I told them we found the poster." She indicated it with a flick of her wrist, seemingly not able to bring herself to look at it. "The policeman said he was – he said he was worried about Hector's having told you what he did," she continued. "They're worried he might realise his mistake and try to leave New York. So they're going up to El Barrio to pick him up now, and then they'll come here to talk to the four of us once they have him in custody." She tried to look at Lydia at this point, but I wasn't sure Lydia had heard a word she'd said.

*

A thin line of reflected blue light hovered at the edge of the windowpane as the police car arrived down below on Fifth Avenue. It must have needed to nudge some traffic out of the way in order to park, because almost instantly we heard the brief discordant wail of its siren – just once, just a single sharp burst; it was almost midnight now, and they obviously didn't want to wake anybody up if they could avoid it.

Marie let them in. The first one was a tall African-American officer in plain clothes; he entered the study with unhurried calm, his red eyes flickering with tiredness, his bald head shining inky black in the glimmers of waxy moonlight. A young white policewoman followed behind him.

"I'm Detective Anderson," the black policeman said. "This is Detective Thorn."

Detective Thorn glanced around the room, her eyes alighting on Lydia, who was staring blankly at them from the sofa.

"This is the poster I told you about," Marie was saying. They both peered down at the desk.

"Right," said Detective Anderson.

Detective Thorn wrote something down.

"Well, we have Mr Soares in custody," Detective Anderson began. "As soon as we mentioned the painting to him, he admitted he did it."

Lydia twisted to face him with an almost violent movement. I may have done something similar myself.

Detective Anderson looked slightly quizzical for a second. "Yeah. He admitted it," he continued. "Totally. Said he did the theft, stole the painting. Sold it. Whole thing."

At that, Lydia began to cry again.

"Are you all right, miss?" asked Detective Thorn.

"I don't know anything about it," said Lydia, through tears. "I don't know anything about it."

"Hmn," said Detective Anderson inscrutably.

Detective Thorn wrote something down.

"Mr... Braeburn?" Detective Anderson said, turning to me.

"Yes," I said, or thought I said. The print was trying to roll itself up on the table. It had freed itself from one of the coasters Marie had placed at its corners to hold it down. The two ends were moving, and suddenly the Devourer's eye came back into view. It glared at me with grotesque absorption. I tried to turn away.

"I believe you were the one to discover all of this, Mr Braeburn?" Detective Anderson was saying.

"I – I was," I said.

"Thank you," said Detective Anderson. "Would you mind coming down to the station house with us for a little while, just to go over a few details?"

"But he..." I said. "But didn't you say – didn't you say that he'd confessed?"

"Sure," said Detective Anderson easily. "But just to tie everything up."

"All the loose ends," said Detective Thorn, looking up from her notebook.

"Dot the 'i's and cross the 't's," said Anderson.

The poster moved again and now I could see the Devourer's mouth. It slowly opened its jaws, its teeth glazed horrifically with thick black saliva.

"Well – yes," I said after a while. "Of course."

The two police officers led me out. Lydia didn't look at me as I left.

*

They drove me with the siren off along the ashen, monochrome uptown streets to a station house on West 67th Street. When we got there Detective Thorn took over, taking note of a few basic details and then leading me down through a warren of tunnels into a dank, scruffy holding cell somewhere deep in the basement, the heavy door closing behind me with an awful and permanent-sounding thud. And then they left me there for two or three hours, a period of time that stretched hideously as I sat slumped at an uncomfortable metal table worrying about what they were going to ask me, whether Hector really had confessed, whether he had tried to tell them it was me. And I worried too about Lydia, her distress in the Peacocks' study, what exactly it meant. And I found myself remembering something she had said at our apartment when I had told her that Hector had threatened me: "It's understandable... It was an important relationship for us both."

I had slipped into a sort of daze of sleeplessness and unease by the time a desk sergeant arrived to say the detectives were ready to see me, and I followed him to an office further down the corridor in something of a stupor. There, Detective Anderson sat weighing up his notes, while Detective Thorn stood beside a high wooden desk writing something down, a shaft of light from a tiny window high up on the wall falling diagonally across her like a sash. And waiting hungrily in the background sat a large, unpleasant-looking white policeman, his bulging eyes baleful and glistening, his whole demeanour chilling, terrifying even. I sat down awkwardly, and I must have been looking pale or nervous because without asking, Detective Anderson poured me a glass of water. Along the back wall ran a line of portraits of past police commissioners, seated and stern, and I guiltily avoided their gaze.

"Sorry to keep you waiting, Mr Braeburn," Detective Anderson said. "We just needed a little time to check a couple of things on our system. It's not exactly state of the art; I think they introduced it right around the time Detective Thorn here was born." The two of them laughed easily. Not the large policeman though.

"So..." said Detective Anderson. "Just to get us started, how about you just run through for us how you discovered this information about Mr Soares," Detective Anderson said.

"Right," I said. "I, well..."

Detective Thorn wrote something down.

I tried to begin again. "I met him in the street," I said.

"You met him in the street," said Detective Anderson. "Now where was this?"

"Spanish – Spanish Harlem," I said. "Where he lives."

"Where he lives," said Detective Anderson. "And what were you doing there?"

"Erm..." I said. "I'd just been out walking – for a stroll... in Central Park. And I wanted to get some cigarettes. So I walked out of the park into Spanish Harlem."

"To get some cigarettes?"

"Yes."

"That's the nearest place?"

"I – From where I was. I think so. Yes."

"Okay. So, you met him in the street. And did you know each other previously to this? Were you meeting one another for the first time?"

"No," I said. "No, but he – he knows who I am. Because he used to be married to – to my fiancée."

"The young lady we met earlier," said Detective Anderson. "Lydia...?" He looked over at Detective Thorn for help. She checked back in her notes.

"Lydia Reis," she said.

"Lydia Reis," said Detective Anderson. "So he knows you because you're dating his ex-wife."

"I'm – she's my fiancée," I said.

"Right. I'm sorry. Your fiancée. You said that. So – who approaches who?"

"He –" I said. "He comes up to me."

"And what does he say?"

"He says –" I could feel my scarab burning in my pocket, the one from the British Museum. I clutched it tightly, begging it to calm the thunderous beating of my heart, which seemed to threaten to betray me at any moment. "He says I need to break things off with Lydia," I said haltingly. "He says I need to leave New York. He says he wants to get back together with Lydia."

"Right," replied Detective Anderson. "And what do you say?"

"I'm not going to leave her. I said I'm not going to leave her."

"Right. And how does he take that?"

"Not very well," I said. "He says to me – he says to me he's dangerous. He said, 'I'm dangerous so – so you better listen to what I say.'"

"'You better listen to what I say'," repeated Detective Anderson. "And what *did* he say?"

"He said maybe I thought – maybe I thought he was just an ordinary guy," I said. "But he's not. He knows some dangerous people and – and he's dangerous, himself. And to show me that, how dangerous he is, he says he's stolen one of the Peacocks' paintings once and – and sold it to one of these – one of these guys he knows. In Spanish Harlem."

"Which painting?"

"I'm sorry?"

"Which painting did he say he'd stolen? Did he know the name?"

"He – he described it," I said.

"And you knew it was this 'Weighing', erm –" He turned to Detective Thorn again.

"'The Weighing of the Heart,'" she said, reading from her notes. "By Edward Hazlemere."

"You knew it was this 'Weighing of the Heart'?" asked Detective Anderson. "You recognized the description."

"Yes," I said. "I knew immediately – which one he was talking about. I used to live there, at the Peacocks'. I was a lodger."

"Yes," said Detective Anderson. "I think you mentioned that to Detective Thorn. So what did you say to him, after that? After he told you about stealing the painting?"

"I – I didn't say anything," I said. "I was scared. I walked away."

"Did he say anything? When you were walking away?"

"Yeah," I said. "He said, 'You better leave her. Because I'm dangerous.'"

"'I'm dangerous'? He said that again?"

"Ah, yeah," I said.

There was a pause. Detective Anderson waited for Detective Thorn to finish writing. She turned a page and came to a halt.

"So when Ms Peacock called us tonight," Detective Anderson said, "I think I said to you, we were worried that he'd regret what he'd said to you and try to get out of town as soon as he could. So we went to see him straight away. He was right there at the address Ms Peacock gave us. We went in, we sat him down, we told him: 'Someone says you took a painting.' You know what he says?"

My mouth was dry. "What?" I said.

"He says straight up: 'Yeah, I did it, I took it, it was me, I acted alone.' Is that right, Detective Thorn?"

She looked back at a previous page in her notebook. "Yeah," she said. "He says: 'I acted one hundred per cent alone.'"

"'I acted one hundred per cent alone,'" repeated Detective Anderson. "I didn't even ask him if he acted alone. I would have asked him, of course," he explained. "But I didn't ask yet, at that time."

"Okay," I said, with difficulty.

"So then I asked him, 'Tell me how you took it.' You know what he says?"

"What?" I managed to ask.

"Nothing," said Detective Anderson. "He says nothing. Just sits there. I ask him again. He says to me, 'Listen. I took it. I'm admitting it. What more do you want?' I say, 'I'm a policeman. I want to know how, where and why.' He says, 'It was me. I took it and I sold it. And I acted alone.'"

There was silence again.

"You ever read any Shakespeare, Mr Braeburn? I'm sorry, of course you do; you're English," he said, before I had had a chance to answer. "Mr Soares, he's very firm on this point, about acting alone. It made me wonder. It got me thinking about Shakespeare: 'the lady doth protest too much.'"

I didn't say anything.

"See, now you're silent too," said Detective Anderson. "Do you think he acted alone?"

I nodded.

"Hmn. So I guess you and Mr Soares agree on that point, anyway," he said.

I didn't say anything.

"Well, let's come back to that," he said. "So you work in an art gallery, I think you told my partner."

"'Latza Art Space'," read Detective Thorn.

"And what do you do at the Latza Art Space?"

"I'm – I'm a junior gallery manager," I said.

"Junior gallery manager," said Detective Anderson. "Right. And you earn approximately...? If you don't mind my asking."

"About – it's about thirty-five thousand a year," I said.

"Okay. And you live with your fiancée, Ms Reis. What does she do?"

"She – well, she worked for a magazine," I said with difficulty. "But – she quit, she quit a few weeks ago."

"Why did she do that?" asked Detective Thorn.

"She – she wanted to – she wanted to concentrate on making prints. She's an artist; she's been working on some prints at the gallery I work at."

"Prints. Like – artworks?" asked Anderson.

"Yes," I said. "That's right. Artworks."

"So, prints, these are, like – for sale?"

"Yes," I said. "Why – why do you need to know all this?"

"Just answer the questions, please, Mr Braeburn," said Detective Thorn mildly. "Are these prints for sale?"

"Yes," I said. "What happens is, you – you have a number of them printed up, like she had a hundred made, and you sign and number each one individually, and then – and then you sell them."

"How much do they go for?" Detective Anderson asked.

"It depends," I said. "But the ones Lydia was making, about two hundred dollars each."

"Okay," said Anderson. "And has she sold many?"

"No," I said. "Not yet. They're not finished yet."

"Oh," he said. "Okay. So as of this moment she hasn't sold any at all?"

"No," I said hesitantly.

"And the two of you live – where?" the large officer asked abruptly, the first time he had spoken. "Oh, no, don't worry, here, I got it," he said, reaching a calloused hand out to take a look at Detective Thorn's notes. "982 Fifth Avenue. Right. So, you're making thirty-five grand a year working in a gallery, she's quit her job so she's actually earning zero right now, so I guess – I mean, I don't live in the city, I live out in Passaic, New Jersey, so, but I guess that address must be down in some inexpensive part of Fifth Avenue, like, erm..." He trailed off.

"It's right by Central Park on the Upper East Side," Detective Thorn said.

There was silence.

"You rent that place?" asked the large officer.

"Yes," I said reluctantly.

"How much does a place like that cost, to rent?"

My heart was beating mutinously in my chest, so loudly I felt sure they could hear it. I fumbled in my jacket pocket for my scarab and I gripped it tightly, and as soon as I did so my heart-rate slowed to a steadier clip, and I was able to reply calmly: "It's rent-controlled. It's twelve hundred dollars a month."

"Pretty good deal," said the large officer, raising his eyebrows. "And I guess your bank records will show this."

My heart began to thump again. I touched the scarab again and the noise ebbed away. "Yes," I said firmly.

"I got to tell you," the large officer said. "I've always been under the impression that it's very expensive to live right by Central Park on the Upper East Side. Like maybe a lot more than twelve hundred dollars a month. Like maybe a guy working in an art gallery making thirty-five grand a year might not be able to afford to live there. Did you... did you come into some money at some point, Mr Braeburn?"

"No," I said.

"Family inheritance? Sale of a valuable item?"

"No," I said, my hand on the scarab.

We were all silent.

"Because we know you've handled valuable items before, don't we, like that ring from that other girlfriend?" asked the large officer. "What was her name?"

"Hannah Martel," said Thorn, reading from a sheet of paper.

I looked up, stunned.

"That's it. Hannah Martel," continued the large officer. "You remember her?"

I was finding it hard to speak. "What?" I said in the end.

"Your name came up on the system," said Detective Anderson reasonably. "No convictions, but there was this one mention, regarding this young lady Hannah Martel..."

"You want me to jog your memory?" the large officer asked me, pulling his chair closer. "That's the one that she breaks up with you because she finds a ring you took, hidden somewhere in your bureau drawer or what have you, starts looking around for what else you might have took, winds up going through all the two of you's bank statements, finds out you drained her life savings out of the joint bank account, flips out and calls the police. Ring any bells?"

I was quiet.

"You leave, you move out, you pay her back, in

the end she tells us don't press charges. You're a lucky man, Mr Braeburn."

"It was just –" I said. "It was all a misunderstanding..."

"Misunderstanding?" the large officer said, moving closer again, his voice rising. "Misunderstanding, like, she thought she loved you, you thought you'd take whatever you could get, because that's the kind of guy you are: you want something, you take it? Right? You don't give a fuck about who it belongs to, you just take it? Is that the kind of misunderstanding we're talking here?"

"No!" I said, standing up. "No. We had – there was a lot of personal stuff going on. She got it all mixed up. It wasn't –"

"All right, Mr Braeburn, all right, all right," said Detective Anderson, palms out. "All right. Okay. Sit down. Relax. Sit back down. Sit down a minute."

Slowly, I sat down, and we were all quiet again for a while. I was breathing hard. Detective Anderson looked through his notes again, and then waved a hand in the direction of the large officer.

"Detective Daley here has been working on a long-running case," he said. "If he doesn't mind, I'll just tell you briefly. For the last few months, he's been trying to build a case against a gentleman named Emilio Ruiz, who we believe has a history of involvement in the fencing of stolen artworks in the city. And the thing why Detective Daley wanted to come in and help us talk to you tonight is because the name of Mr Soares recently came up in his case, that maybe Mr Soares is someone who might have recently supplied a painting for Mr Ruiz in this line of work. You following me, Mr Braeburn?"

I knew I ought to reply to this but I couldn't seem to do it. In the end, I just nodded.

"Is that something you know anything about, that kind of thing?" asked Detective Daley.

"What – kind of thing?" I asked with difficulty.

"Fencing stolen paintings," he said. "And that kind of thing?"

"Me? No," I said. "No. No."

They were all looking at me. There was a long period of silence.

"I mean you can understand why I'm asking," said Detective Daley eventually. "Here's a guy, you work in the art world. Living well beyond your means. Very unclear your true source of income. And plus, when we look into it, there's some sort of history here of – never comes to court, but it seems like theft to me, this thing with the other girlfriend. I'll be honest with you, Mr Braeburn, I don't know what's going on here, and I don't know how exactly you fit in with Mr Soares and Mr Ruiz, but the one thing I am one hundred per cent sure of is that you do fit into it somewhere. You do fit into it somewhere."

He looked up at Detective Anderson intently. "You know it's your call, Detective," he said to his colleague. "It's your call. I know that. But in my experience in this profession, you get white guys from the Upper East Side who are mixed up in this kind of shit they are not mixed up at the bottom, they are mixed up at the top. All right? So I say let's fucking get Hector in here and see who out of these two guys can keep his story straight. All right? Let's bring Hector in here and then let's find out exactly who's telling the truth and exactly who this kid is and what he's really been doing. What do you say, Detective?"

Anderson looked at Detective Daley, and then back at me, watching me closely, unblinking and still, and then he turned away and started rifling thoughtfully through his papers and notes until he had half of them in one hand, half in the other. He looked up at Thorn for a second, and then looked meditatively back at his papers. Thorn held her pen poised above her notepad; she seemed to be watching him for some kind of signal. There was a pause, during which Daley coughed roughly and then shuffled slowly across the floor towards a packet of cough sweets on the desk, his trunk-like legs peculiarly out of step with his body. He ponderously unwrapped one of the sweets, and then threw it into his mouth, crunching it violently, and then he looked round at me suddenly with frank ravenousness, his yellow tongue rotten and foamy, his deep-set green eyes voracious, insatiable – and suddenly it was the Devourer looking at me, it was the Devourer sharpening its knives as my life lay in the balance, and I slapped my pockets, unsure for a moment which one held my scarab, but I found it, and I gripped it tight. I turned towards Detective Anderson, and he was adjusting the scales weighing my heart against the feather, his black jackal's head gleaming lasciviously, his red eyes narrowing. I tried to concentrate on what he was doing, but I couldn't take my eyes off the Devourer, the harsh folds of its scaly skin, the teeth longer than the height of its snout, jutting like daggers, glistening in the pitiless sunlight. Anubis let go of the scales, Thoth watching intently, and my heart and the feather beside it sank and swayed, up and down, as they began to find their true level. My ba murmured worriedly at my ear, my heart dipped lower and lower... guilty, it was saying, I was guilty – guilty of the theft, of setting Hector up, of lying to Lydia, of betraying the Peacocks, of stealing from Hannah... I clasped my scarab tightly, painfully, trying desperately to make it silence my heart, and my scarab burned in my hand, so hot now that a small plume of smoke was beginning to rise from it. The Devourer rocked back on its haunches, ready at any moment to launch itself forward and plunge its teeth into my neck – and then the plume of smoke from the scarab gently reached the smoke alarm in the ceiling and a cacophonous siren split the room.

Detective Anderson looked up. The frightened face of an officer had appeared at the small square window in the door. "Fire!" he was yelling. "In the cells! There's thirteen people locked down there." Anderson flung open the door as three officers raced past.

"I've got the code," one of them was shouting. "I need that key from the –"

"Fire! Fire!" another one yelled as he sped past. "This ain't a drill!"

Detective Daley's eyes were darting from me to the gathering chaos outside and back.

"Daley!" someone shouted. "Got the key to the –?" The rest was inaudible.

"Huh?" yelled Daley.

"We need the key! There's thirteen suspects –"

One of the officers barrelled into the room, another close behind him, and they grabbed the key from Detective Daley. And suddenly we were swept up in the tide of police officers rushing along the corridor outside, and somewhere between that flight of stairs and the next, I found myself separated from Anderson, Thorn and Daley and shepherded upstairs by a terrified-looking young policeman, obviously a new recruit. On the sidewalk outside, I paused for a moment to look at the burning station house, flames squalling behind silhouettes at the windows, as two fire engines skidded to a halt in front of its doors. Then I turned and hurriedly followed my ba east along 67th Street towards the park and towards our apartment.

*

It was pitch-black as I struggled through the pathways of the park, but my ba was glowing freely now and it lit my way. Behind me, rising and falling in intensity, I could hear a terrifying lurching sound, the footsteps of something large and ungainly – but every time I turned around, I could see nothing through the dark splinters of the trees and the rocks.

I turned off from the path and started towards Sheep Meadow, glancing behind me briefly as I pushed my way through the harsh thickets, and as I did so, just for a moment, the yellow eyes of the

231

Devourer blinked rapidly in the darkness of the undergrowth behind me. I struggled on through the bushes, but as I broke free of their branches and ran out across the meadow I saw a silhouette matching me pace for pace in the darkness to the south – stumpy back legs, careening front paws, and that ugly, pointed snout pushing its way towards me through the night...

At the other side of the meadow, I clambered unsteadily over the wall of the park and out on to Fifth Avenue, a clanking noise coming from somewhere behind me as I raced through the fury of the car horns. On the corner before my block, I turned to see yellow eyes hurtling towards me like spears. The scales had fallen. My heart was too heavy. I was guilty. It would find me.

I hurried into the lobby of our building and flung myself into the elevator, slamming my palm against the door button again and again until it closed, sinking down against the wall once the doors had shut and I was safe. Lydia would help me. She would know what to do.

*

The apartment was silent when I got in, so quiet I felt I could hear the ticking of the digital clock displays and the glacial running of the glass in the windowpanes. I walked from room to room, out on to the flat roof and back – but she was nowhere to be seen. The sulphurous lights of the skyscrapers drifted gradually back into the blue dawn behind me.

I called her and it went straight to answerphone. I sent her a text message; after a while, I sent her an email. Then I called her again. I sat on the bed. Something about the flat itself told me that she had gone for good, a quality of stillness, a settling of the dust in the rooms as if everything she had ever touched had now finally stopped moving forever. I could feel nothing where she used to be, and inside my chest, a gasping, vacant hollow was beginning to open up as my body, seemingly before my mind, began to understand this. My skin felt rumpled and loose. My eyes were swaying with fatigue. The Devourer had killed her, I realized suddenly. This was how my punishment would start – it had taken her life before it could take mine.

Oh God... I doubled up on the bed, paralysed with loss, and felt suddenly the things I would never feel again: the spark of her fingers, the warmth of her arms around me in the mornings, her energy and restlessness. I knew that I knew her, down to the bones, that I would always know her, and that she knew me. Two artists, alone.

Oh God... Holding her at night, wanting and being wanted in those quiet, sleeping hours, the city still and silent around us. Her hair curling out wildly in the morning like a lion's mane. My hand on the back of her neck, on the curve of her hips. Her laughter, her smile when she was mocking me, the gleam in her eye, that scatter of auburn across her irises like the Milky Way. The glow in her cheeks. We were two points on a line, looking at each other along the line. We had fused ourselves together, and I didn't know how I was going to begin to disentangle what was me and what was her. The pillows on our bed still smelt of her, and I pushed my face deep into the fabric to get what I could.

When I looked up, I stopped still. In the darkened doorway to the kitchen were two gleaming yellow eyes. I stayed exactly where I was. Had it seen me? It wasn't moving. But it must have seen me. That was why it was here. It had killed Lydia and now it was going to kill me. The scales had come down...

But perhaps it wasn't too late. Perhaps I was wrong. Perhaps it hadn't killed her. Perhaps she was on her way to Portugal, to Lisbon – perhaps she was waiting for me there, and I pictured her talking happily in Portuguese, safe, warm...

And perhaps I could still get out, too, perhaps I could join her there, perhaps I could escape –

perhaps that would be our own Field of Reeds.
Perhaps it wasn't too late.

Carefully, slowly, never taking my gaze from
those bloodshot yellow eyes, I backed away from the
bed, and forced myself up. I pulled my passport and
my money silently from the drawer of the bedside
table and shoved them into my pockets, and
continued to back away, keeping my eyes at all times
on the Devourer, my ba carefully unlocking the
apartment door behind me. But at the sudden click
of the lock, the Devourer's head shot up – and at
once it was bounding out of the kitchen into the
light towards me, blood and saliva from its fangs
splattering across the bed, across the floor.

I scrambled to the door, my ba screaming in
panic, and scuffled through, slamming it hard
behind me. The door jumped and rattled in its frame
as the Devourer threw itself at it again and again in
fury and frustration.

Not daring to wait for the elevator, I ran down
the hallway and into the stairwell, the steel door
banging behind me, and raced down the eleven
flights of stairs, pushing my way through the
unwieldy emergency doors into the lobby. Crying,
breathing madly, on the verge of a panic attack or
perhaps in the middle of one, I struggled out on to
Fifth Avenue and flagged down a cab, the streets

flashing by in a tear-stained blaze of turquoise and pink neon, my ba whipping ahead of the cab and then back to my side in loops of fear.

I scanned the pavements and the streets and the cars around us and the boats in the water below as we crossed the bridge above Randall's Island and headed towards JFK – was it there? Was it there? But I could hardly see. The streets were pitching and yawing before me, the rivers, the bridges, the buildings and the reflections of the buildings. My vision was flooding white, then black, then red, then white...

But I could do it. I had to do it. I would catch the first flight I could, the huge frozen rivers unfurling below me like hieroglyphs as I headed north over Canada, up above the whole conjoined American continent to Portugal, safe above the clouds, above the rain, above the weather, above the seasons and sunsets, cut loose from the earth turning slowly below me – scraped raw by the raw sun.

Chapter 11

I live in a small complex of buildings now on the Atlantic coast in South Carolina, in a place that unlike New York City has neither scale nor size, not really – a tiny dab of orange tilework among the lush green of the forests and the swirling, darkling blue of the sea.

I like the evenings best here, when I can smell the dinner cooking, and hear the sounds from the back yard where some of the others sometimes play baseball. There's a dog that must belong to a family a few miles from here, and from my open window, I like to watch him spend the last hour or two before sunset chasing his tail up and down the muddy track that runs behind the buildings, just outside the fence. I find it a good time to sit and think – peaceful, still, nature stretching and reshaping itself as day slips slowly into night, the crickets, the birds, the whispering leaves in the trees. I sit drinking a glass of water and listening to the sounds of the game as the sun sinks down into the hills behind me, its last rays spreading quietly over the rooves of the town below and the estuary leading languidly out towards the sea.

I feel a lot calmer these days. I work a few hours a week in the workshop designing tiles that are sent down to a store in Atlanta – it's the nearest thing to artwork I do now – and there is a French doctor here who has put me on what seems to me to be a good regime. I sleep well, I rarely dream, I go for walks around the grounds and to the part of the fence that is on a slight incline, where you can see people from the town take small boats out sailing if the weather is fine. Sometimes they dive off the back of their boats, and occasionally I'll see a woman whose wet brown hair glistens against her back just like Lydia's, and I'll close my eyes and their voices will fade and I'll hear Lydia's voice instead.

I'm not allowed to phone her, or email her, of course, and I'm not quite sure what I would say now even if I could, so much time has passed. But last year they began to allow me limited access to the internet and from then on, from time to time, I would do Google searches for Lydia Reis, and Hector Soares, and Edward Hazlemere and 'The Weighing of the Heart.' And, with the exception of one brief local news report from 2012 explaining the outcome of the trial, nothing would ever come up.

But then suddenly, earlier this year, a few months ago, a link appeared for the first time when I typed in her name: a small gallery, not the Latza but something called the Putnam Collection, was selling three works by an artist named Lydia Reis: 'Queen Nefertiti', 'The Barque of Ra', and 'The Lake of Fire.' I clicked on the tiny thumbnail image of 'The Barque of Ra' and it expanded to fill my screen. The boat, sketched in with little more than two or three lines. Ra resplendent, first as a falcon and then as Khepri. The Field of Reeds lush, welcoming and cool, foliage bending softly in the breeze. And at the centre of the image that huge, hypnotic sun, bursting as brightly from the monitor as it had from the small frame in Rose Peacock's bedroom. There was no further information underneath the image, but when I searched through the gallery's website, I found a single line in a long alphabetical list of names: 'Lydia Reis is a Portuguese artist who was born in Lisbon and studied fine art at New York University.' And I stared at that line gratefully for a long time, enjoying the feeling of the word 'is'.

And in the afternoons, when I walk back home along the dirt track from the workshop, pushing myself steadily through curtains of rain, rivulets of water dripping impassively down my face, I imagine her, still and always the age she was when I met her, almost seven years ago now, living out a long life happy and warm, perhaps back home, back in Lisbon at last, sitting sipping coffee with friends and family at a cobblestone café beside the deep, raging currents of the Tagus, working intently in a crowded, sunlit studio on beautiful new pieces about the mutu and the ka and the Field of Reeds, looking exactly as she did when I first saw her slipping across the roof garden in the darkness that night, her eyes gleaming in the reflected light from the laundry room like a cat's, the way she was, the way she always will be, forever.

And I imagine that perhaps one day we will meet again, travelling to the other side, our scarabs secure in our hands glowing and gold – and I will reach out my fingers towards her and she will take my hand, and she will feel the pulse in my veins as my heart beats for her, steadfast and loyal, and I the pulse in hers as her heart beats for me. And we will rise up and follow the path of the ba I saw that morning on the window ledge as she slept softly and peacefully by my side.

Acknowledgments

With thanks to everyone who helped me get this book into its finished state, including: Eleanor Long, Sue, Tudor and Sian Owen, Rachel, Adam, Ben and Amy White, Gerda Ismay, Nicola Barr, Theo Bishop, Andrew Bowers, Mike Brophy, Ruth Brown, Ada Calhoun, Caroline Chatwin, Catherine Cranston, Charlotte Davies, Ben Evans, Joe and Beth Garrod, Dave Gatrell, Rhona and Jon Grifflow, David Grossman, Maggie Hanbury, Glyn and Anna Huelin, Eszter Karpati, Matt Keating, Brent Korson, Kieran and Lizzie Kumaria, Zoe Marks, Jim McKenzie, Jamie McLaughlin, Catherine McShane, Helene Mulholland, Elena Passarello, Sarah Phillips, Anna Pickering, Harriet Poland, Alan Simpson, Jack Smyth, Anthony Vigor, Arnold Vis, Lewis Williamson, Louis Wood, Chris Wright, Gotham Writers, and M.W. Leeming and Nathan O'Hagan of Obliterati Press.

About the author

Paul Tudor Owen was born in Manchester in 1978 and was educated at the University of Sheffield, the University of Pittsburgh, and the London School of Economics.

He began his career as a local newspaper reporter in north-west London, and currently works at the Guardian, where he spent three years as deputy head of US news at the paper's New York office.

If you enjoyed this title, follow Obliterati Press on Twitter and Facebook for details of forthcoming releases.

@ObliteratiPress

Also, be sure to check out our website for regular short story contributions.

Also available from Obliterati Press:

LORD OF THE DEAD

Richard Rippon

A woman's body has been found on the moors of Northumberland, brutally murdered and dismembered. Northumbria police enlist the help of unconventional psychologist Jon Atherton, a decision complicated by his personal history with lead investigator Detective Sergeant Kate Prejean.

As Christmas approaches and pressure mounts on the force, Prejean and Atherton's personal lives begin to unravel as they find themselves the focus of media attention, and that of the killer known only as Son Of Geb.

Also available from Obliterati Press:

THE BAGGAGE CAROUSEL

David Olner

Dan Roberts has a troubled past, anger management issues and a backpack named after an abducted heiress. A chance encounter with Amber, a free-spirited Australian girl, seems to give his solitary, nomadic life a new sense of direction. But when she doesn't respond to his emails, the only direction he's heading is down…

The Baggage Carousel is a visceral yet humane travelogue of a novel about life's great let-downs; family, work and love. Dan Roberts is destined to go down as one of fiction's great solitary men, equal parts Iain Banks' Frank, Camus' Meursault and Seuss' The Grinch.

Also available from Obliterati Press:

WE KNOW WHAT WE ARE

Russ Litten

We Know What We Are is the debut short story collection from novelist Russ Litten, author of *Scream If You Want To Go Faster, Swear Down* and *Kingdom.*

This batch of tense and edgy tales are all centered in and around Hull in the year 2017 and feature a cast of citizens whose lives play out in the furthest edges of the City of Culture spotlight.

Also available from Obliterati Press:

SUNSET TRIP

Ben Vendetta

It's 1999, and former music journalist Drew, out of rehab, is trying to hold down a soul-sapping day job, and struggling to come to terms with another failed relationship. Reconnecting with a musician friend, Drew is given the chance to relocate to L.A. and a path back into the music industry. But will this move be Drew's last shot at contentment, or will it drag him back into the rock'n'roll heart of darkness?

"Take the expressway to your skull as Ben Vendetta delivers another lysergic slab of subcultural mayhem, oozing with unabashed style and pizazz in *Sunset Trip*! A tale told thru the rhythm, chronicling life in the peripheries of endearing veteran indie rocker geek, Drew. Set amidst the fallout years of the shoegaze scene (psychedelia's last gasp) as the original indie epoch bids farewell to the 20th century in a cataclysmic cloud of hedonistic chaos! Will Drew get out alive, or end up behind the cemetery gates pushing up psycho daisies? Vendetta's magnum opus is realised from the inside looking out, depicting a world now far from view, though still 'too real to feel'."
— Sam Knee, author of *A Scene In Between*.

CPSIA information can be obtained
at www.ICGtesting.com
Printed in the USA
LVHW110328011019
632710LV00001B/99/P